SAN TALES

FROM AFRICA

RAFFAELLA DELLE DONNE

ILLUSTRATED BY MARJORIE VAN HEERDEN

SAN TALES

FROM AFRICA

CONTENTS

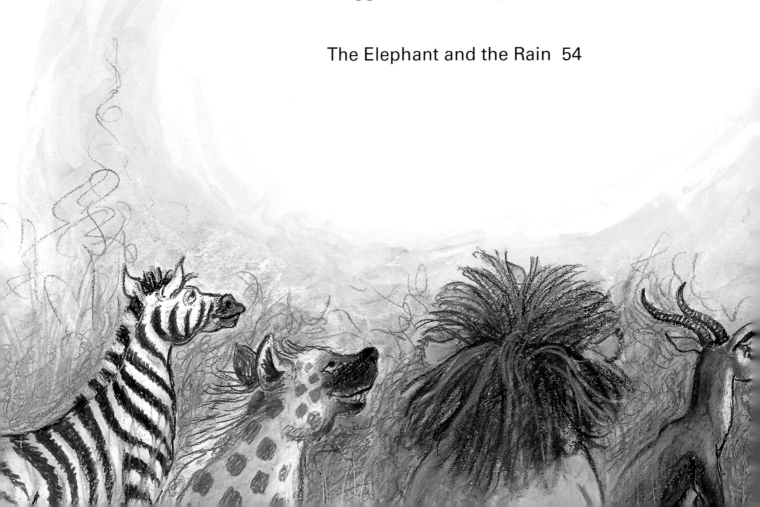

INTRODUCTION

My first encounter with San mythology was as an undergraduate student of archaeology at the University of Cape Town. In my final year, inspired by numerous field trips to the Cederberg, I specialised in mythology and rock art. I began my research by drawing up an inventory of all the animals that appear in San mythology, as well as a description of how each animal features in the stories. Initially, I was extremely frustrated at having to do something so tedious!

For weeks I sat in the university's African Studies Library, trying to make sense of the stories told to Wilhelm Bleek and Lucy Lloyd in the early 19th century. (Bleek, a 19th-century linguist who came to live in South Africa, was the first to write down the /xam language with the help of his sister-in-law, Lucy Lloyd. San prisoners, of whom there were many at the time, were released into their care and lived with them in Mowbray, Cape Town, so that they could record their stories, which appear in a collection entitled *Specimens of Bushmen Folkore*.)

Because the myths were told and translated word for word in an attempt to record San language, the stories seemed to me fragmented, repetitive and incoherent. However, the longer I spent immersing myself in the world of the First People, the more I began to understand the language and the style of the stories. Through these stories, I met an array of fantastic characters that were simultaneously kind, daring, mischievous, bad-tempered, violent, rude, clever and helpful. There are no inherently good or bad characters in San mythology; I think that is why the stories appealed to me so much. I have adapted and re-told these stories for a number of reasons, first and foremost to keep the art of African myth-making and storytelling alive.

As a child growing up in South Africa, my imagination was dominated by European fairy tales in which princesses needed rescuing from castles and gingerbread men were eaten by witches. Today, our children grow up with similar stories or, even worse, Disney versions of their African heritage.

Although these San stories appear in the form of a children's book, it is by no means implied that the myths and their characters are the product of a childlike imagination. In fact, many of the stories were meant for an adult audience. Despite their seemingly simplistic nature, the stories are infused with meaning related to the San's religious and social life. Many of the stories are about the First People, or People of the Early Race who existed before the San. The San do not have a myth of beginnings the way many other cultures do, but believe rather that the world, as they know it, unfolded slowly as a result of many incidents.

The central character in San folklore is the trickster god, whose name varies according to each linguistic group. In this collection, the /Xam name, |Kaggen is used (although please note that in the stories themselves |Kaggen will simply be spelt as 'Kaggen', i.e. without the '|'). In the /Xam language, |Kaggen is pronounced by first producing the dental click that is signified by the '|'. According to Mathias Guenther's book on the San entitled *Tricksters and Trancers*, this click can be pronounced by positioning the tip of the tongue against the upper incisors to create a sound that is similar to 'tsk, tsk' (i.e. a sound that might be used to scold a child). It is common for the letter 'k' to appear after a click, and was described by Dorothea Bleek, who continued her father's work of recording the /Xam language, as a 'very loud plosive croak'. The 'g' is pronounced in the same way as 'k', and 'e' is similar to the English use of the vowel as in 'bed' or 'tent'.

In San folklore, the trickster god appears as a praying mantis and, during the colonial period, Europeans mistakenly thought that the San worshipped the mantis. This is because, according to San cosmology, |Kaggen, the trickster god, transforms himself into a mantis to communicate with the San. |Kaggen is an ambiguous and contradictory god. He is simultaneously the creator and destroyer of all things. He can be extremely wise and moral, but also rude and greedy.

In the popular imagination, myth continues to be associated with either the past or the fictitious, but the most characteristic feature about myth is its refusal to simply go away. Why? Because myth is not, essentially, about the past, nor is it about characters and events that did not actually exist. Myth tells us about our present and, yes, even our future. The power of storytelling lies in its ability to create a world without the boundaries, rules and limitations of this world, allowing us to challenge and dream of a better world. I see myth as an important tool for keeping African culture and heritage alive in the popular imagination, and to challenge the idea of San culture as 'extinct' and 'primitive' and therefore not part of present-day South Africa.

The preservation of San heritage is not merely about museum displays and recreations of rock art for tourist-related merchandise. It should also be about the telling of their stories. It is only through the telling and re-telling of stories that San mythology can be kept alive in the consciousness of all South Africans, both in the present and in the future.

KAGGEN AND THE ALL-DEVOURER

This story does not form part of the mythology, but was inspired by many of its characters.

There was a time, a very long time ago, before you or I were born, when only the First People roamed the earth. But unlike any people whom you might know today, the First People were actually animals. Not ordinary animals – they wore simple clothes and could talk, sing and dance. In fact, they could do just about anything you or I can do. Some of the First People even had magical powers.

The praying mantis, whose name was Kaggen, had extraordinary powers. He could make himself invisible. He could even grow feathers and fly when he needed to make a quick escape from trouble. For, you see, this insect had a habit of finding himself in trouble. He was the most curious and most mischievous of all the First People. He liked nothing better than to spend his day playing tricks on others or solving a mystery. That is why it was Kaggen who was chosen to seek out the All-Devourer when the great darkness began to cover the earth.

One day, the All-Devourer, who was said to have no arms or legs, and who lived at the bottom of the river, began swallowing all the plants and trees on the earth. But he didn't stop there; when all the plants and trees had been eaten, he ate all the rocks and the mountains. Still not satisfied, the All-Devourer began to swallow all the stars in the night sky and finally even swallowed the sun and moon!

Eventually, the elders of the First People met under the dark sky, not knowing if it was morning or night. It was decided that young Kaggen should be sent to find the All-Devourer and try to find a way to return the sun, moon, stars, plants, trees, rocks and mountains to the First People. Kaggen felt very proud to be chosen for this important mission, but he was also anxious.

'It is so dark without the sun, moon and stars,' thought Kaggen, 'how will I find the All-Devourer?' And, he wondered, how could a tiny insect like himself possibly stop the All-Devourer who must surely be huge? As these questions filled his head, Kaggen prepared for the long journey ahead. After bidding farewell to all his friends and family, Kaggen called to his belongings to follow him: 'Come along, Shoes! We're on our way, my trusty friend,' he said poking his Bag. 'No more lying around, Walking Stick, we have a job to do!' Up jumped the Shoes and the Walking Stick and began to follow swiftly behind Kaggen. They were soon followed by the heavy Bag, who moved a bit more slowly because he was filled with Kaggen's belongings for the journey.

With each step he took, it seemed to Kaggen that it was becoming darker and darker. 'This darkness is no good to us,' he complained to his belongings. For, you see, not only could they understand Kaggen, but they could even talk back!

'We need to find the Ostrich,' said the Bag in a slow, deep voice. 'It is said that the Ostrich carries the secret of fire …'

'What good is fire to us?' interrupted Kaggen before the Bag could finish, for he was sometimes an impatient fellow.

'Oh, be quiet and let him finish speaking, Kaggen!' exclaimed the Walking Stick, who was the cheekiest of all the belongings.

'It is no ordinary fire that the Ostrich carries. It is the secret to making a fire that never goes out,' explained the Bag.

'Ooh! I know! I know!' yelled each of the Shoes, jumping up and down. 'If we find the secret fire, then we will have light to see our way through the darkness.'

'Exactly,' said Kaggen smugly, as if it was his idea all along. 'Well, what are we waiting for?' he added. 'We have wasted enough time with your jabbering.' And before any of Kaggen's belongings could ask how they were going to find the Ostrich, they were on their way again.

After a few minutes, Kaggen tripped over something round and hard. Thinking it was a rock, Kaggen angrily picked it up and was about to throw it when the rock let out a yelp. Kaggen immediately dropped it and saw that this was no ordinary rock. It had a head, four short legs and even a tail. This was no rock at all, silly Kaggen! It was the Tortoise.

'Sorry about that, Tortoise,' apologised Kaggen.

'Don't worry, young Kaggen,' replied the old Tortoise, 'I'm often mistaken for a rock.'

Chuckling, the Tortoise asked, 'Now tell me, Kaggen, what mischief are you up to today?'

Kaggen held his head up high, puffed out his chest and replied in a proud voice: 'I am on a quest to find the All-Devourer.'

The old Tortoise began to howl with laughter: 'Well, well, young Kaggen. How are you going to find the All-Devourer if you can't even tell a Tortoise from a rock?'

Indignant, Kaggen told the old Tortoise about his plan to find the Ostrich who, he had been told, had the secret to make fire that would never go out.

'It just so happens,' whispered the Tortoise in a soft voice, 'that I know where Ostrich keeps her fire.'

'Tell us! Quickly, tell us. You must tell us at once!' demanded the Shoes. They were very excited at this news.

'Patience, my friends. If I tell you where Ostrich hides her fire, what will you do for me in return?' asked the shrewd Tortoise.

'Anything!' Kaggen, the Stick and the Shoes all replied in unison.

The Tortoise was very pleased to hear this. He replied, 'Very well, friends. Just give me a moment to think about it.' And with a large grin, the Tortoise's head disappeared back into his shell.

'I wonder what that crafty old Tortoise will make us do?' asked the Walking Stick in a bit of a huff. Of all Kaggen's belongings, he hated to be kept waiting.

'Shhhhh', hushed the Shoes, 'he'll hear you.'

Quietly, they all waited around the Tortoise until, finally, they saw his wrinkled head pop out of his shell.

'That's settled then. All you have to do, my young friends, is to help me win the race against Ostrich tomorrow,' said the Tortoise gleefully.

'A race? You against Ostrich?' wailed Kaggen. 'But that's impossible.'

The Tortoise flashed Kaggen another one of his bright, mischievous grins: 'That's precisely why I need your help, Kaggen. Ostrich is so vain and boastful. She always makes fun of me for being slow. I think it's time that she is put in her place, once and for all.' He chuckled to himself: 'I can't wait to see Ostrich's face when I tell her we are going to be racing each other tomorrow.' However, when he saw how worried Kaggen looked, the tortoise stopped laughing. 'You are a smart one, little mantis. I know you will think of something,' he said, as he slowly disappeared into the darkness.

'Don't worry, Kaggen,' chirped the Shoes, lighting up when they saw Kaggen's long face, 'we will come up with a plan.'

'It is useless,' muttered Kaggen shaking his head. 'Did you see how slowly the Tortoise moves? He will never win the race against Ostrich.'

Then the Bag, who had been quiet for a very long time, said in a slow, deep voice: 'The fastest runner doesn't always win the race, Kaggen.'

They all stared at the Bag in disbelief, and then the Shoes and the Walking Stick began to roar with laughter: 'Did you hear that? The fastest runner doesn't always win the race. Ha! Ha! Hee! Hee!'

Suddenly they realised that Kaggen wasn't laughing. Instead, his frown had been replaced by a large grin. 'He is right! The only way we will help Tortoise win the race is by using our heads,' said Kaggen. 'And I, my friends,' he said rubbing his hands together, 'have a plan up my sleeve for tomorrow's race.'

Just then, the Walking Stick yawned widely, which made everyone realise how tired they were. Tomorrow was going to be a big day, and they all needed as much rest as possible. Within a few minutes Kaggen was fast asleep with his head on the Bag, the Walking Stick by his side and the Shoes snoring gently at his feet.

In the morning, Kaggen woke up to find himself being poked by the Walking Stick. Muttering something about tortoises, Kaggen rolled over and went back to sleep. 'Ouch!' The Walking Stick had poked him even harder. 'Stop that. I'm awake,' cried out Kaggen.

'I'm glad to see you are awake, Kaggen,' came the voice of the Tortoise. 'Now, I want to know how you are going to help me win the race against Ostrich. Tell me quickly.'

Kaggen rubbed the sleep out of his eyes, sprang out of bed excitedly and began whispering his plan into the Tortoise's ear, fearing that the stones might hear and would tell the Ostrich. The Tortoise began to chuckle as he heard Kaggen's plan, and was still chuckling as he slowly made his way to the Elephant's waterhole where the race would begin. Kaggen and his friends knew they had no time to waste, and went about their business quickly to make sure that everything went according to plan.

When Kaggen arrived at the Elephant's waterhole he found the Ostrich there already, stretching her long legs in preparation for the race. 'Are you here to watch me win the race, Kaggen?' asked the Ostrich, fluttering her long eyelashes.

'Oh yes, I have come to watch the fastest bird in the land,' said Kaggen slyly, for he knew how much the Ostrich liked to be praised.

'Stop boasting. You haven't won yet, my dear,' said a croaky voice. It was the Tortoise. He had been there all along, cleverly hidden among the tall reeds.

'Come on, let's get on with it, then,' said the Ostrich, tossing her head in the air and fluffing out her feathers.

The Ostrich and the Tortoise took their place at the start of the Elephant's waterhole, and when Kaggen gave the signal to begin, the Ostrich raced

off, leaving behind a cloud of dust. As they watched the Ostrich disappear into the distance, Kaggen and the Tortoise grinned at each other. In the meantime, the Ostrich had slowed down a bit, thinking that she must be far ahead of the old Tortoise. But then suddenly, just in front of her, she saw the Tortoise plodding along slowly.

'That can't possibly be Tortoise ahead of me!' cried out the Ostrich, and she began to run faster to overtake the Tortoise. After a few minutes, she saw the Tortoise again. Just ahead of her. The Ostrich took a deep breath and began to run even faster, because now they were close to the finish line. With every long stride she was getting closer and closer, when suddenly she saw the Tortoise again. He had just crossed the finish line. Tortoise had won the race!

The Ostrich was furious. She began to stamp her feet angrily, kicking up so much dust that she didn't see Kaggen and his friends rolling around on the ground with laughter, delighted that their plan had worked. With a loud huff, the Ostrich stormed off and then, one by one, all the Tortoises who had been hiding among the reeds began to appear. Kaggen had tricked the Ostrich by asking all the other Tortoises to hide in different places until they saw her coming closer. The Ostrich couldn't tell one tortoise from another so, no matter how fast the Ostrich ran, it seemed as if the Tortoise was always ahead of her.

'Thank you, Kaggen,' said the Tortoise. 'That is one the finest tricks I have ever seen,' he added, wiping the tears of laughter from his eyes. 'Now I will tell you where Ostrich keeps the secret of fire.' The old Tortoise leaned closer, so that his head was almost touching Kaggen's. Everyone gathered around, anxious to hear Tortoise. He whispered: 'The secret of eternal fire is hidden under Ostrich's wing. She guards her secret very closely. That is why Ostrich never lifts her wings. She's afraid someone might see the glow.'

Kaggen was overjoyed. Now they could continue with their quest. He called his belongings together and immediately set off in search of the Ostrich. It wasn't long before Kaggen spotted the Ostrich, dancing by the glow of a fire. Seeing her dance gave Kaggen an idea of how to steal her secret.

'Good evening,' said Kaggen as he crept nearer to the Ostrich.

'Eeek!' shrieked the Ostrich. She didn't expect anyone to be there, and immediately stopped dancing.

'No, please don't stop, Ostrich.' Kaggen stepped into the light. 'You look so beautiful dancing by the light of the fire,' said Kaggen. Delighted, the Ostrich blushed and fluttered her long eyelashes at Kaggen, who then smiled slyly and quickly added: 'But I hear that your sister, Crane, is the most beautiful dancer in the land.'

The Ostrich stamped her foot, her eyes flashing angrily: 'How dare you, Kaggen! Can't you see for yourself that I am a more beautiful dancer than my sister, Crane?'

'Please don't be angry with me, fair Ostrich,' said Kaggen smoothly. 'Dance for me again, so that I may tell everyone I meet that I have seen you, and that you are by far the most beautiful dancer in the land.'

The Ostrich was overjoyed. 'At long last, everybody in the land will know that I am the most beautiful dancer,' thought the Ostrich to herself and so she began to dance.

At first she only used small movements, but as Kaggen's clapping and cheering became louder and louder, so her movements grew wilder and wilder. Kaggen waited until she had lifted her wings high enough and he could see the soft glow of the secret fire. At just the right moment, Kaggen jumped up, snatched the secret fire and fled as fast as he could. As Kaggen disappeared into the darkness, he could hear the angry screams of the Ostrich. Kaggen ran faster and faster. The screams of the Ostrich became fainter and fainter. When he was sure that he couldn't hear the Ostrich anymore, Kaggen stopped to rest in the tall grass.

'Is it safe to come out yet?' whispered the Bag.

'I'm not scared of Ostrich,' scoffed the Walking Stick, even though he was brave enough only to poke out his head.

The Shoes giggled, then asked the Walking Stick: 'Then why are you still hiding?'

The Walking Stick was just about to give the Shoes a hard tap for being so cheeky when Kaggen jumped up and said: 'Stop quarrelling and look around you.' Kaggen was holding out the magic fire, and they were surrounded by the most beautiful light.

'Wow.' whispered the Shoes, their eyes wide in amazement.

'We'll have no trouble seeing our way now,' said the Bag cheerfully.

'That's certainly true,' replied Kaggen, 'but I think we should rest for a while longer.' It had been a long day, and the poor little mantis was very tired.

As Kaggen lay down on his back looking up at the sky, he wondered how they were going to find the river where the All-Devourer was said to live. 'There are so many rivers in our land,' Kaggen said to his belongings, 'we can't possibly travel to every river looking for the All-Devourer. By then the All-Devourer would have swallowed everything, including ourselves!'

The Shoes began to tremble as they imagined themselves being swallowed up by the All-Devourer. For a long time they were all silent. Only the Walking Stick paced up and down, as he always did when he was thinking about something important: 'Tap, tap, tap.' Kaggen grew more and more irritated.

'Walking Stick, will you stop your pacing! How am I supposed to rest with all that noise?' yelled Kaggen finally.

The Walking Stick began to sulk and muttered under his breath: 'Maybe the Rain will know where the All-Devourer lives. She is friends with all the rivers of the land.'

Kaggen's face lit up: 'Of course! Of course the Rain will know,' he exclaimed, jumping up. 'Come on, what are we waiting for?' he said to the Walking Stick, who lay on the ground without moving. He called to the Walking Stick again, but the Walking Stick refused to budge.

'I'm not moving until you say you are sorry for yelling at me,' said the Walking Stick.

'All right, I'm very sorry,' said Kaggen, bowing his head.

'Good. Now you can thank me for giving you the idea to ask the Rain where the All-Devourer lives,' said the Walking Stick with a smug smile.

Kaggen was furious, but he swallowed his pride and said through gritted teeth: 'Thank you for your splendid idea, Walking Stick. Now, can we go?' he asked. And, with that, they were off again, leaving the tall grass whispering to the wind.

After a little while, in the distance, Kaggen and his friends heard a slow but loud rumbling sound. The Shoes began to tremble: 'Wh... Wh... What's that noise?' they stammered.

Whatever it was, it was moving closer. Suddenly they heard the sound of laughter high up in the sky. 'Oh, dear little Shoes,' said a kind voice, 'don't be afraid.'

They all looked up at the sky and saw that it was the Rain. Kaggen grew feathers and, clutching his belongings, flew up, high up into the clouds closer to the Rain. 'That is my cousin, Thunder. He only sounds scary,' the Rain said to them. The Shoes were not convinced at all, and huddled closer to each other. Suddenly there was a deafening crack and the sky was lit up by a brilliant streak of light. 'Ah, my cousin Lightning. Now *that's* who you should be afraid of, my little friends,' said the Rain to the Shoes.

But the Shoes were nowhere to be seen. 'Where could they be?' exclaimed Kaggen.

'Ha! Ha!' scoffed the Walking Stick. 'Look at the Bag, look how he is shaking. Aren't you a bit old to be scared of thunder and lightning?'

'Mmmfh! I can assure you, I'm not afraid of a little thunder and lightning. But I do believe there is something inside me that is making me tremble.'

Kaggen peered into the Bag and, sure enough, there were the Shoes, shaking with fear. They had been so scared by the arrival of Lightning that they had jumped into the bottom of the Bag!

'I think the Shoes are ready to get back onto solid ground. Don't worry my friends, we will be on our way soon,' chuckled Kaggen. Then, turning to the Rain, he said: 'Rain, I was told that the All-Devourer lives at the bottom of a river. There are so many rivers in the land. It will take far too long to search every river. We need to find the All-Devourer and stop him before there is nothing left to swallow!'

The Rain smiled at Kaggen and replied: 'Don't worry, brave little Kaggen. My cousin Thunder will be able to help you. He'll tell you where you can find the All-Devourer.'

In the meanwhile, Kaggen and his friends were still walking among the clouds. They waited eagerly for Thunder to tell them where they could find the river where the All-Devourer lived. They waited while Thunder scratched his chin for what seemed to be a very long time. Finally, in a loud booming voice that stretched across the sky, Thunder said: 'The All-Devourer lives in the river that runs through the forest of the Rainbull.'

'Who is the Rainbull and how will we find him?' wailed the Shoes.

'Oh, little Shoes! Don't you know anything?' asked the Walking Stick. 'The Rainbull lives in a dark forest and he is said to be very, very grumpy. You must be careful not to make him angry, because if you do, he will turn you into a frog.'

'A frog?' whispered the Shoes to each other. Poor little Shoes, they looked so afraid. Thunder thought this was extremely funny, and the sky was filled with the sound of his roaring laughter.

'Don't worry, little ones,' he said, kindly, 'I will ask my sister, Lightning, to send a message to the Rainbull asking him to help you. She will make sure that the Rainbull is expecting you,' said Thunder, his voice growing softer and softer as he disappeared into the distance. Kaggen and his friends stared at the sky until they could see no trace of Thunder, before making their way to the forest of the Rainbull.

It wasn't long before Kaggen could see the long, winding river that ran through the forest where the Rainbull was said to live. 'Come on, friends. We are almost there,' Kaggen said happily, for he could see that his belongings were tiring. As they drew closer to the river, Kaggen noticed that the trees were growing very close together. Before long they were almost surrounded by trees so tall that they couldn't see the sky any more.

'Oomph!' groaned the Bag suddenly. The Walking Stick had stopped quickly, without any warning, causing the Bag and the Shoes, walking behind him, to bump into each other.

The Walking Stick whispered: 'Ssshh, I think I hear something.' They were all quiet. And then, out of the darkness, appeared two red eyes.

Trying not to be scared, Kaggen stepped forward and puffed out his chest: 'My name is Kaggen. I am on a quest to seek the All-Devourer that lives at the bottom of the river,' he said in a loud voice. But the two eyes didn't move. Kaggen cleared his throat and tried again: 'My name is Kag... ' But before he could finish his sentence, he heard a peculiar noise that sounded like a mixture of a choke and a cough. Stepping even closer to the red eyes, Kaggen saw the most extraordinary sight. A bull, the colour of the sky at midnight, was lying on his side and he was ... laughing!

'You're ... you're Kaggen?' asked the Rainbull in between fits of laughter. Before Kaggen could reply, he added: 'How is a little praying mantis like you possibly going to stop the All-Devourer?'

The Shoes, who had been hiding behind Kaggen, looked up and saw that Kaggen was no longer afraid. He was angry. 'Please don't be angry, Kaggen,' begged the Shoes from behind his legs. 'We don't want him to turn us into frogs,' they said before disappearing again.

'The Shoes are right,' thought Kaggen to himself. He took a deep breath and said: 'Well, Rainbull, are you going to help us, or not? I was chosen to stop the All-Devourer, and I will do it, with or without you.'

Hearing Kaggen's words, the Rainbull got up and dusted himself off. 'My, my, you are a serious young fellow.' And then, with a snort, he added: 'I would not be so cheeky if I was you, my young friend. You will need my help if you are to reach the bottom of the river where the All-Devourer lives.'

Kaggen did not like being scolded. He was just about to tell the Rainbull that he didn't need his help when the Rainbull jumped into the river and called out to Kaggen: 'Oh do stop sulking, and climb on my back. I will take you to the bottom of the river.'

But once Kaggen saw how dark and deep the river was, he did not feel so brave after all. Staring at his own reflection in the water, he said: 'Rainbull is right; I'm too small to stop the All-Devourer. He must be huge.' No sooner had Kaggen spoken these words than he noticed a big, dark shape in the river.

'Th-the-there he is,' stammered the Shoes in fright.

'I wouldn't stand so close to the edge if I was you,' warned the Rainbull. And with a squeal, the Shoes jumped into the Bag.

The Walking Stick, who had been resting quietly on the ground, suddenly leapt up into the air and tapped the Rainbull on the shoulder: 'Pardon me, but aren't we forgetting about one small problem?'

'And what's that, Walking Stick?' asked Kaggen, trembling. He was becoming more and more afraid.

'You are a mantis. You can't breathe under water,' said the Walking Stick smugly.

This was all too much for the poor little mantis. 'It's hopeless,' he cried, falling to the floor with his head in his hands.

'Don't give up now, Kaggen. There must be a way,' said the Bag. He didn't like to see Kaggen so sad.

'Kaggen might not be able to breathe under water, but I can, and as long as he stays on my back, he will too,' said the Rainbull, looking very pleased with himself. Then, turning to Kaggen, he said, 'Well, my little friend, what do you say?'

Kaggen looked into the river again and then up at his friends. They were all watching him intently as they held their breath, waiting to hear his answer. 'Well, what are we waiting for?' asked Kaggen, pretending to be far braver than he felt as he jumped onto the Rainbull's back. He'd never been under water before. But all Kaggen's belongings huddled away from him on the river's edge and said nothing. 'What's the problem now? No, wait, let me guess, you don't want to get wet?' Before any of them could reply, Kaggen continued: 'That's all right, my friends. It will be very dangerous, and it's better that I go alone.' The Shoes began to cry.

'There, there, little ones. Nothing is going to happen to Kaggen,' said the Bag softly.

'Go get him, Kaggen!' chimed in the Walking Stick. And, with that, the Rainbull disappeared under the water with Kaggen holding onto him as tightly as he could, leaving the Shoes, Bag and Walking Stick at the edge of the river. As they went deeper and deeper under water, Kaggen's eyes grew wider and wider. He could hardly believe his eyes. The river was empty! There were no fish or crabs. There were no plants. There weren't even any rocks.

'You see, Kaggen,' said the Rainbull looking over his shoulder, 'the All-Devourer has eaten everything in the river.'

Suddenly, something caught Kaggen's eye. It was a small head. 'Surely that can't be the All-Devourer?' he asked the Rainbull.

'Take another look, Kaggen,' replied the Rainbull. And so Kaggen did. What he saw was a tiny head stuck to a huge sleeping body. His enormous body was covered in rolls of fat that quivered in the water.

'The All-Devourer,' whispered Kaggen, for he did not want to wake him. As the All-Devourer snored, Kaggen watched the huge body move up and down.

'He is so fat. He looks as if he is going to burst,' said the Rainbull quietly. This gave Kaggen an idea.

'Hurry, we need something sharp. Help me find a stone before he wakes up,' whispered Kaggen into the Rainbull's ear. Quietly they swam away and began to search for a sharp stone. But the All-Devourer had swallowed everything in sight.

'This is hopeless,' said the Rainbull, ready to give up.

'Wait, I have another plan,' said Kaggen. He was a determined little mantis! 'Rainbull, let me use one of your sharp horns to cut open the stomach of the All-Devourer.'

A big grin came over the Rainbull's face as he said: 'Kaggen, I am sorry I laughed at you. You might be small, but you are a clever fellow.' The Rainbull's words made Kaggen blush and he looked down shyly at his feet. 'Here you are, my brave friend,' said the Rainbull.

Kaggen looked up. The Rainbull had put one of his horns into his hands. Without wasting any more time, they swam quietly towards the All-Devourer, taking care not to disturb him. When they were close enough to the All-Devourer so that Kaggen could feel his breath on his face, Kaggen leaned over and sliced open his stomach. And with that, everything that the All-Devourer had swallowed jumped out of the hole in his stomach. Open-mouthed, Kaggen and the Rainbull watched as fish, bees, zebras, baboons, giraffes, stones, plants, snakes, owls, trees and finally, the moon, the sun and stars, all came rushing out.

'I think we'd better leave now, Rainbull!' shouted Kaggen over the stampede, 'We must go before the All-Devourer discovers that it was us who sliced open his stomach.'

The Rainbull nodded his head: 'Yes, I think you are right, Kaggen. Hold on, here we goooo!'

Faster and faster swam the Rainbull. Poor little Kaggen was so exhausted, but he kept holding onto the Rainbull's back for dear life. At last they reached the edge of the river, and waiting there were the Shoes, Bag and Walking Stick.

'Kaggen!' they all cried out. They were so happy to see him that tears of joy rolled down their cheeks.

'Well done, my friend,' said the Bag in a slow, deep voice.

'You did it!' squealed the Shoes.

Kaggen beamed at his belongings: 'Thank you, my friends. Oh thank you. But I couldn't have stopped the All-Devourer without the help of the Rainbull.'

'That may be so, but where is the Rainbull?' asked the Walking Stick, spinning around.

'Mmm … that's odd. He was here a moment ago,' replied Kaggen, looking around.

'Can we go home now, Kaggen?' asked the Shoes.

'I suppose we can, little ones. Oh, I do wish the Rainbull had said goodbye,' said Kaggen, patting the Shoes.

'We didn't even have a chance to say thank you,' said the Bag, softly.

The Walking Stick, who was now very anxious to go home, tapped on the ground and said: 'Come along then; we can't stand around waiting for the Rainbull. It is going to be a long journey.'

Kaggen was also looking forward to returning home to his friends and family, but he was sad to leave without saying goodbye to the Rainbull. Slowly, they began to make their way through the forest. 'I wonder what became of the All-Devourer?' thought Kaggen to himself. And then, just as they were about to leave the forest, they heard a peculiar noise. 'I know that noise!' exclaimed Kaggen. And sure enough, the Rainbull appeared, laughing as he waved goodbye to Kaggen and his friends.

'Goodbye!' yelled the Shoes, jumping up and down.

'Thank you for all your help,' added the Walking Stick.

'What does the Rainbull have on his back?' asked the Bag.

Kaggen squinted to have a better look. 'Why, it is a frog!' he said.

'A frog?' asked the Walking Stick.

'Kaggen, you don't think that could be the All-Devourer, do you?' giggled the Shoes.

Kaggen gave a smile and said, nodding his tiny head: 'It just might be, my friends, it just might be.'

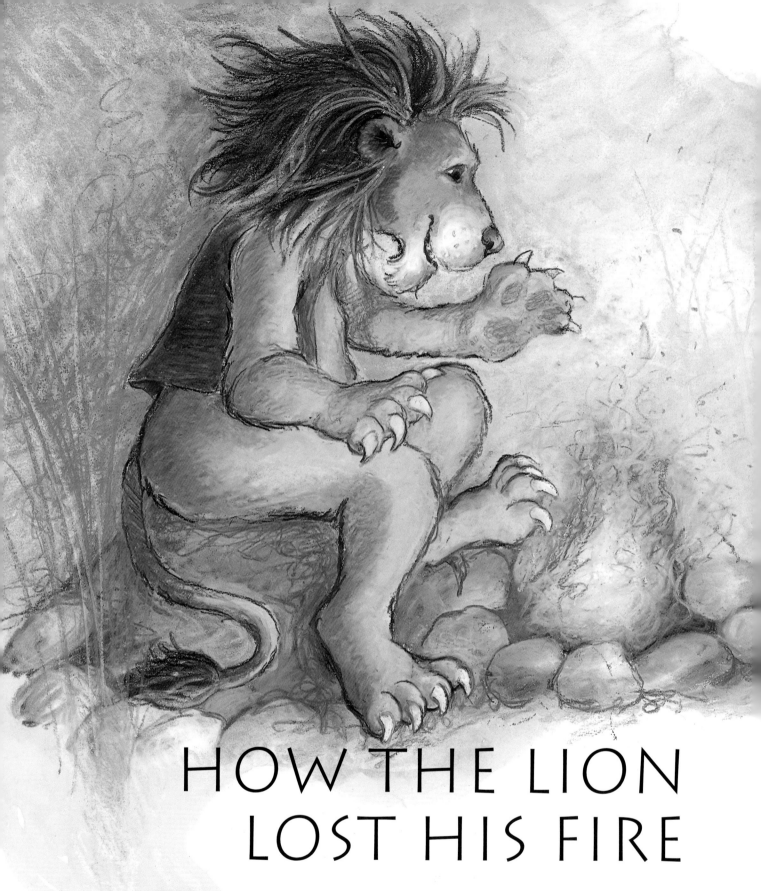

HOW THE LION LOST HIS FIRE

A story based on the version that appears in Folktales of the Kxoe in the West Caprivi,
Christa Kilian-Hatz (1999). Rudiger Koppe Verlag: Cologne.

During the time of the First People, when people were animals, the Lion was a grumpy old man. He was the only one who knew how to make fire, and would not share his fire with anyone else. One day, all the animals decided to find a way to steal the fire from the Lion. They also wanted to have a nice, warm fire to sit around at night. On that day, all the animals were up before sunrise and gathered together early in the morning. It was decided that the Giraffe, because she was the tallest and could see everyone properly, should be in charge of the meeting.

'All right everybody, settle down,' the Giraffe said to the other animals, for they were all talking excitedly among themselves and were being very noisy indeed.

The Dassie was the first to speak. 'The Lion is the fiercest animal in the land. How will we ever take the fire away from him?' she asked.

Suddenly, all the animals began to speak at once. 'Everyone be quiet!' cried out the Giraffe over their heads. 'We will never have fire if we do not listen to each other and work together.'

All the animals became quiet when they heard what the Giraffe had to say. 'Giraffe is right, we must all give each other a chance to speak,' said the wise Tortoise. 'I have an idea,' he added. 'I will wait until Lion is sleeping in the sun, and then I will very quietly creep close to the fire and steal it away. He will not even notice me because of my shell.'

A big grin spread over Jackal's face. 'Old Tortoise is right! Because of his shell, it is easy for him to hide among the rocks and plants.'

All the animals began nodding to each other and, before long, it was agreed that the Tortoise should be the first to try and steal the fire away from the Lion.

Just then, a little voice high up in the tree said: 'I can help too.' Everyone turned around and looked up. It was the Bush-Bird: 'I can fly ahead and let Tortoise know when Lion is asleep.'

The Giraffe said: 'I think that's a fine idea, Bush-Bird. Well done!'

All the animals let out a cheer and called out: 'Hooray for Bush-Bird and Tortoise!' This made both Bush-Bird and Tortoise blush. There was much excitement and chatter among the animals as they waved goodbye to the Tortoise and the Bush-Bird. Perhaps, by that night, they would all have fire, the animals thought to themselves.

As it grew closer to midday, the sun became hotter and hotter. From a safe distance, the Bush-Bird watched the Lion, who was lying under the shade of a big thorn tree. Before long, he yawned loudly and his eyes began to close. When it seemed as if the Lion was nearly asleep, the Bush-Bird flew back to the Tortoise's hiding place and whispered: 'Okay, Tortoise. Now is your chance.'

The Tortoise gave the Bush-Bird a wink, and began slowly, and steadily, to make his way to where the Lion was sleeping. The Tortoise would take a few steps, and then pull back into his shell, just in case the Lion woke up. Every now and then the Lion stirred. The Tortoise then kept very still with his head and legs hidden inside his shell. It was not too long before the Tortoise had moved close to the Lion and his fire. When he was close enough, the Tortoise reached out and grabbed the fire. But just at that moment the Lion woke up, and noticed that his fire was not where he had left it.

'That's strange,' thought the Lion, as he looked around and saw that his fire had been moved and was lying next to a rock. Of course, it was not really a rock. It was the Tortoise who was keeping very, very still. Luckily for the Tortoise, the hot sun was making the old Lion lazy, and when he could not see anyone else around, he closed his eyes and went back to sleep.

The Bush-Bird, who had been keeping watch all that time, flew up to the Tortoise and whispered: 'You can come out now, he is asleep.'

The Tortoise let out a big sigh as his head popped out his shell. Poor little Tortoise was so scared when the Lion woke up that he had been holding his breath all that time.

'Hurry Tortoise!' exclaimed the Bush-Bird, who was fluttering around him. Once again, the Tortoise began to slowly and quietly move away from the sleeping Lion. He had only moved a few steps when the Lion was suddenly woken up by a little fly sitting on his nose. The Bush-Bird quickly flew to tell the Tortoise, but it was too late. The Lion had already spotted the Tortoise.

He let out a big roar and called out: 'Where do you think you are going with my fire?' The Tortoise was so frightened that he dropped the fire, pulled back into his shell and rolled under a rock where the Lion could not reach him. The Lion grabbed the fire and, marching off, he said: 'The fire belongs to me, and I am not going to share it with anyone.'

As soon as the Bush-Bird saw it was safe to leave her hiding place, she quickly flew back to where all the other animals were waiting.

'Well, Bush-Bird, did the Tortoise get the fire?' asked the Springbok. But all the little bird could do was shake her head sadly as she told the animals what had happened.

'Maybe someone who is much faster than the Tortoise should try to take the Lion's fire,' suggested the Baboon, scratching his head.

The Giraffe looked around at all the animals. 'What about you, Duiker?' said the Giraffe, pointing her long neck at the little buck. The animals let out a big cheer at the Giraffe's suggestion. They were sure that the Duiker could steal the fire away from the Lion. She was small, but everyone knew she was fast!

The Duiker felt very shy, but she stepped forward and, in a soft voice, said: 'Very well, friends. I will try my best.'

And with those words, the little buck disappeared in a cloud of dust with the Bush-Bird not far behind.

After a short while the Monkey, who had climbed high up in the trees, cried out: 'Hey, everybody! I think I can see Duiker coming.' All the animals gathered around the Monkey.

'Does she have the fire?' asked the Giraffe excitedly, stretching her long neck to take a better look. Sure enough, it was the Duiker, running very quickly towards them. But to everyone's dismay, the Duiker did not have the fire.

'Oh, no,' wailed the Field Mouse, who had been looking forward to warming his whiskers at the fire. When the Duiker arrived, she was so out of breath that she could not even speak.

Before she even had a chance to say anything, the Hyena said in a loud voice: 'So, not even Duiker was fast enough to snatch the fire away from that grumpy old Lion.'

The Hyena's words made the Duiker's eyes fill with tears as she said: 'I am so sorry, I have let you all down.'

The Giraffe looked at the Hyena and, in a stern voice, said: 'Now look what you have done, you have made poor little Duiker feel sad when you are not even brave enough to try and steal the fire yourself.'

This made the Hyena feel very ashamed and, without another word, he slunk off with his tail between his legs.

By now, the animals had begun to think they would never take the fire away from the Lion. They were all very quiet. 'Come on, friends! We must not give up now,' said the Giraffe with her head held high.

Then the Eland stepped forward and said loudly in a proud voice: 'Giraffe is right. We must try again. I will go and steal the fire away from the Lion.'

And with those words, the Eland ran off. But it was not long before the Eland also returned empty-handed. One by one, each animal had a turn, but none of them could prise the fire away from the Lion. As the day wore on, the animals lost all hope. Even the Giraffe could not think of anything to say to make them more cheerful. When it was almost dark, the Ostrich was the only one left who had not yet had a chance.

'The day is not over, friends. I will try and steal the fire,' said the Ostrich to the animals who were all looking very glum.

'Why even bother, Ostrich?' sighed the Bush-Bird. 'I have seen everyone try and fail. The Lion is too fast and clever.'

Fluffing out her feathers, the Ostrich said: 'But everyone has had a chance. What makes you think that I cannot take the fire?'

All the animals began to laugh at the Ostrich. 'Do not be so silly, Ostrich. No-one has been able to do it, and neither will you!' said the Monkey, who was laughing the loudest. The Ostrich was very angry at the other animals for laughing at her. She stamped her foot hard into the ground and said: 'You just wait and see.'

The next morning, the Ostrich woke up very early and set off to find the Lion. She did not have to look for very long before she spotted him warming himself in the sun. She crept up to the Lion as quietly as she could and grabbed the fire. Startled, the Lion jumped up and chased after her. But just before the Lion had time to snatch the fire back from the Ostrich, she did a very clever thing! The Ostrich used the Lion's fire to light the nearest tree. When the Lion saw what the Ostrich was doing, he roared: 'No! Come back with my fire!'

But the Ostrich kept running and lighting every tree and bush she could see, spreading the fire more and more. Just as the Lion came near the Ostrich, she dropped the fire. It was too late, now there was nothing the Lion could do. The Ostrich had started too many fires! He could not possibly snatch them all. The Lion let out such a deafening roar that the rest of the animals came running out to see what all the noise was about. To their delight, they saw fires everywhere.

'Ostrich has done it! She has stolen Lion's fire!' cried out the Giraffe. 'Come on everyone, grab a fire.'

And, while the Lion ran from one fire to another, each animal snatched a fire before running as far away from the Lion as they could.

'Well done, Ostrich!' all the animals cried out together. The Ostrich had never felt prouder in her life. From that day on, everyone had a fire to keep them warm at night, but the Lion never stopped trying to steal his fire back. And that is why, to this day, the Lion still chases after all the other animals.

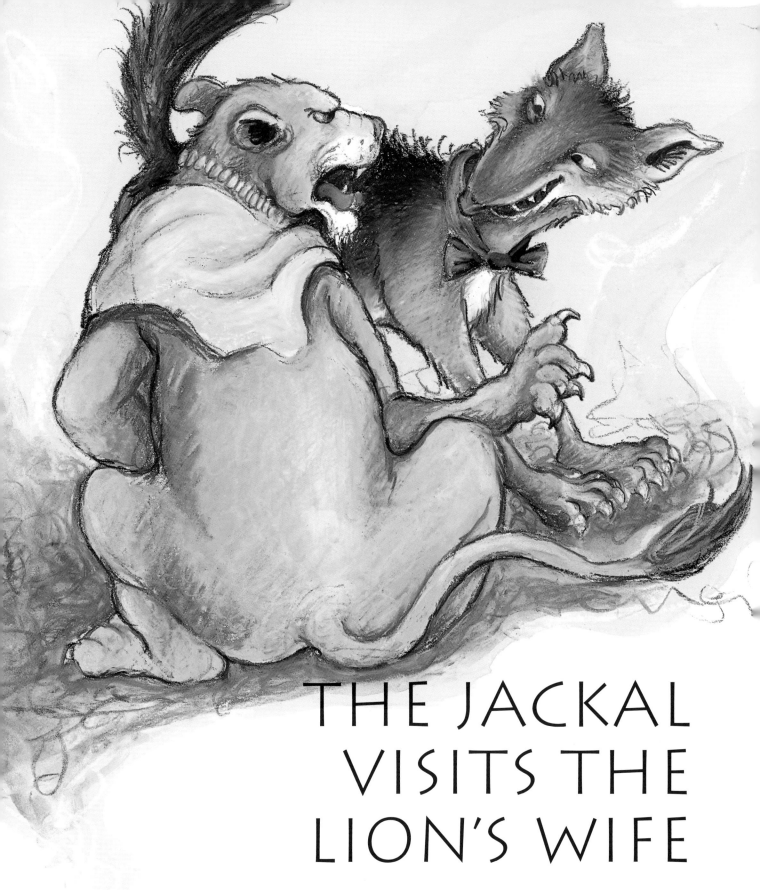

THE JACKAL VISITS THE LION'S WIFE

A story based on the version that appears in Bushman Stories, *E.W. Thomas (1950).*
Oxford University Press: Cape Town, London, New York.

A long time ago, the Lion and his wife were the proudest and vainest of all the First People until, one day, the Jackal came to visit and taught them a lesson. Everyone was afraid of the Lion and his wife, except for the Jackal. He was a crafty fellow, and knew that he could outsmart them. And so the Jackal decided to pay the Lion's wife a visit. When he arrived there, he walked straight into the Lion's house without even a knock on the door.

'I demand to know where Lion is,' the Jackal called out loudly in a haughty manner.

The Lion's wife was very angry when she saw the Jackal standing in her house. 'How dare you!' she roared. The Jackal gave a big grin and sat down, putting his feet on the Lion's favourite chair. He did not look at all afraid.

'First you come in without knocking, and then you speak to me so rudely,' the Lion's wife said to the Jackal and tried to grab him. But the Jackal slipped out of her reach as quick as lightning. This made the Lion's wife even angrier.

'I demand to know where Lion is,' said the Jackal once again. And then, with a sly smile he added: 'Lion is my servant, you know.'

The Lion's wife made another grab for the Jackal, but he ducked and ran between her legs. Her eyes were red with anger: 'My husband is not your servant. He is the strongest and fiercest in the land!'

The Jackal ran out of the door as fast he could and looked over his shoulder as he called out: 'Lion is my servant! Lion is my servant!'

The Lion's wife chased after him. Once outside, she saw that the other animals had come out to see what all the noise was about. 'Everyone has heard the Jackal say that my husband is his servant. I am so ashamed,' she thought to herself.

When the others heard the Jackal, they all began to laugh. 'Ha! Ha! Lion is Jackal's servant,' they said to one another. 'Lion must be very afraid of Jackal!'

Monkey, who was laughing the loudest of all, called out to the Lion's wife: 'So that must mean that you are married to Jackal's servant!'

The Lion's wife ran back into the house in shame when she heard the animals laughing. 'As soon as my husband comes home, that Jackal is going to pay for what he has done!' She paced up and down all day as she waited for the Lion.

The sun had set by the time the Lion returned home. He was tired after a long day of hunting, and was happy to be home. He found his wife waiting at the door, fuming with anger. She stamped her foot and roared. Before the Lion could even ask her what the matter was, she asked him: 'Have you heard what everyone is saying about you?'

The Lion gave a big yawn and answered: 'No, I have not, and whatever it is, I am sure it can wait until tomorrow.'

The Lion's wife cried out: 'You old fool! Something must be done today. Everyone is laughing at you behind your back. They say that you are Jackal's servant.'

Poor Lion. All he wanted was some peace and quiet. He sighed: 'Calm down, my dear wife. Who really cares what Jackal has said?' Then he added: 'Anyway, everyone knows that I am the strongest and fiercest in the land.'

But the Lion's wife was too proud to allow the Jackal to make her feel so ashamed in front of the others. She knew that her husband was also very proud, so she said: 'All the other animals have been saying that you are afraid of Jackal.' She could see that this annoyed the Lion as he began to feel angry. 'No one will ever be afraid of you again,' she added under her breath.

'What did you say?' roared the Lion.

The Lion's wife looked away and smiled to herself and said: 'Oh nothing, husband. Just talking to myself.' The Lion's wife knew just what to say to make her husband really cross.

The Lion gave another loud roar: 'I heard what you said. I am going out right now to find Jackal.'

The Lion's wife was pleased that the Lion was going to do as she asked, but she let him think it was his idea. 'You are so brave and clever, my dear husband,' she said, as she stroked his mane.

This made the Lion puff out his chest and say: 'I know I am, and now I must be off.' And with a flick of his tail, the Lion left to find the Jackal.

It was already dark when the Lion left his house and most of the animals were fast asleep. 'Where is Jackal?' the Lion cried out and then roared loudly into the night sky. One by the one, some of the animals woke up.

'Did you hear that?' whispered the Hare to the Porcupine, who lived next door. The Porcupine was so scared when she heard the Lion's roar

that she began to tremble. 'L-Lion is f-furious,' she stammered, 's-someone must w-warn J-Jackal.'

The Porcupine was too afraid to look for the Jackal herself. She did not want to run into the angry Lion, so instead she went to find the Hyena who lived close by. When she arrived, the Hyena was already awake. 'Did you hear the Lion's roar, too?' the Hyena asked her, wide-eyed with fright.

The Porcupine nodded and then said: 'We must help Jackal.'

'But how will we do that?' asked the Hyena.

The Porcupine answered: 'I have a plan. You must find whoever lives closest to you. Tell them that Lion is looking for Jackal, and they must pass on the message.'

The Hyena grinned and said: 'I see, so everyone keeps passing the message on until it reaches Jackal.'

The Porcupine nodded her head so furiously that all her quills shook: 'Yes, exactly! Now run along, we cannot waste any more time,' she said to the Hyena.

And so the Hyena slunk off into the darkness to find the Ostrich and her sister, the Crane. As soon as the Hyena had told the Ostrich and the Crane, they hurried off to tell the Giraffe. The Giraffe told the Springbok who then told the Zebra, and so it went, until finally the Monkey found the Jackal fast asleep in the bushes.

'Wake up, Jackal. Lion is looking for you and he is very angry,' the Monkey whispered into the Jackal's ear.

The Jackal yawned and did not even open his eyes. 'Leave me alone, Monkey. I'm not scared of that silly old Lion,' he mumbled and tried to push the Monkey away. The Monkey jumped up and down around the Jackal until he opened his eyes. 'All right, Monkey. I am awake, stop that!' grumbled the Jackal. He got up and dusted himself off.

Suddenly, they both heard a loud roar. The Jackal turned to the Monkey and whispered: 'You were right, Monkey. Lion sounds very angry.' But the Monkey was nowhere to be seen. When he heard the Lion coming, he ran up the tallest tree he could see. 'Coward!' Jackal called out to the Monkey. 'Lion may be stronger and fiercer than me, but I am cleverer than that old fool,' the Jackal said to himself. 'I just need to find a way to trick him.' It was not long before the Jackal had thought of a plan. Quickly he set off to find the Bees. He was going to need their help.

When the Lion found the Jackal, Jackal pretended to be sound asleep in the bushes. 'Wake up!' the Lion roared, but Jackal did not even move or open his eyes.

All he said was: 'Lion, is that you?'

'If you opened your eyes you would see that it is me,' said the Lion angrily. But still the Jackal did not open his eyes. 'Why is Jackal keeping his eyes closed?' thought the Lion to himself. Lion threw back his head and gave another loud roar. 'Open your eyes!' he yelled.

Jackal answered: 'Do not be angry. I cannot see, Lion. The Bees stung my eyes because I tried to steal their honey.' The Lion began to feel sorry for the Jackal, but then he remembered what Jackal had done. However, before the Lion had a chance to comment, the Jackal said in a soft voice: 'Please do not hurt me, Lion. I was wrong to have shamed you and your wife. Let us go to your house and I will beg her to forgive me.'

When the Lion saw how sorry the Jackal was, he thought to himself: 'Poor Jackal, I think he has already learnt his lesson.' The Lion turned to Jackal and answered: 'Very well, Jackal.'

The Jackal tried to hide a smile from the Lion and said: 'I will not be able to find my way, you must carry me on your back.' The proud Lion did not want to carry Jackal all the way home, but he could not think of another way to take him there. And so the Jackal climbed onto the Lion's back, feeling very pleased that his plan was working.

The rest of the animals were very surprised when they saw the Lion pass by, carrying the Jackal. They were curious to find out why the Lion would do such a thing, so they decided to follow them. 'Maybe Lion really is Jackal's servant,' said the Porcupine softly so that the Lion would not hear.

But the Hare knew better and said: 'No, Jackal must have tricked Lion. I hope we find out what the Jackal is up to.'

No sooner had the Hare said those words than suddenly they heard the Lion scream with pain: 'Ouch! Ouch!'

The animals rushed to see what was happening and there they saw the funniest sight. The Lion was being chased by the Bees while the Jackal was on his back holding tightly on to the Lion's mane, trying hard not to fall off. The animals did not know that Jackal had asked the Bees to help him.

The Lion's wife came out of the house when she heard her husband screaming and could not believe her eyes. There was the Lion running with the Jackal on his back while the Jackal cried out: 'Faster! Faster!'

She called out to her husband: 'So Jackal was right, you really are his servant!' The poor Lion tried to explain to his wife why the Jackal was on his back, but she did not believe him.

'What Bees? I do not see any Bees!' she said angrily. By then, both the Bees and the Jackal had disappeared. The animals looked on and laughed when they saw how the Jackal had tricked the Lion and his wife once again.

When the Lion saw that the Jackal was gone, he knew that the Jackal had told him a lie. Both the Lion and his wife were so ashamed that the Jackal had been clever enough to trick them twice that they were never as proud and vain again.

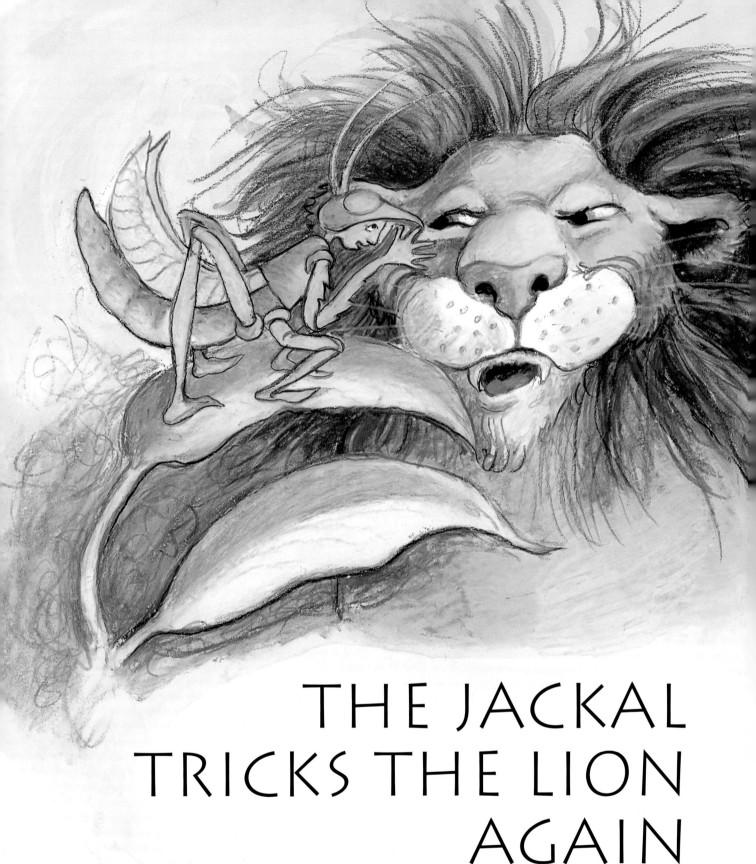

THE JACKAL TRICKS THE LION AGAIN

A story based on the version that appears in Living Legends of a Dying Culture, *Coral Fourie (1994). Ekogilde: Hartbeespoort.*

One day, Kaggen came across the Lion who was lying with his chin on his paws, looking very glum.

'Hello, Lion, is there something the matter?' asked Kaggen. The old Lion gave a big sigh. Kaggen sat down next to him and said: 'Tell me what it is. Maybe I can help.'

The Lion looked at Kaggen with big, sad eyes and answered: 'I feel lonely, Kaggen. I do not have any friends to hunt with me.'

Kaggen pinched the Lion's cheeks and said: 'Cheer up, old boy. I will go hunting with you.'

The Lion growled at Kaggen. He hated having his cheeks pinched. 'Leave me alone, you rascal,' said the Lion and lifted his big paw.

Kaggen jumped back when he saw the Lion's sharp claws and said: 'All right, all right. There is no need to bite my head off.'

The Lion lay back down with his chin on his paws. He let out another big sigh and said: 'Anyway, you are far too small to go out hunting with me, Kaggen.'

'I may be small, but I am a good hunter!' exclaimed Kaggen. This made the Lion roar with laughter. Kaggen folded his arms and started to sulk, but the Lion was not paying any attention. Something in the distance had caught his eye. Kaggen saw that the Lion was watching the Jackal, who was out hunting for food.

The Lion jumped up and said: 'There is Jackal, I will ask him if he wants to hunt with me.'

This time it was Kaggen's turn to laugh. 'You old fool,' he said as he rolled about on the ground laughing, 'everyone knows that you cannot trust Jackal.'

The only thing the Lion hated more than having his cheeks pinched was someone laughing at him. He let out such a huge growl that Kaggen could see all his teeth, and he stopped laughing. 'I am sorry for laughing, Lion. I was only trying to help you,' said Kaggen, standing up.

The Lion shook his mane: 'Run along, little mantis. I do not need your help.' And with that he turned his back to Kaggen and walked away.

'That's fine with me, but you will be sorry that you did not listen to me!' Kaggen called out after him. The Lion did not even turn around to answer him.

When the Lion found the Jackal, he was lazing in the sun. 'How is the hunting going today?' the Lion asked the Jackal.

The Jackal looked up, but the sun was in his eyes, so he could not see who it was. Squinting slightly, he lifted a hand to shade his eyes and asked: 'Is that you, Lion?'

The Lion answered: 'Yes, it is, Jackal. I saw you hunting earlier. Have you had any luck?'

The Jackal stretched and yawned: 'Not yet, so I thought I would have a little rest and try again later.' The Lion did not know that Jackal was very lazy, and would rather spend his days lying in the sun than be out hunting. The old Lion should have listened to Kaggen's warning. For,

you see, the Jackal did not really hunt that much himself and would steal food from the other animals whenever he had the chance.

The Lion said to the Jackal: 'I am looking for a friend who will hunt with me.' The Jackal was surprised, because he knew that the Lion was a good hunter and did not need any help.

'Perhaps I can find a way to steal some food from Lion,' thought the Jackal to himself. 'But Lion, why do you need my help?' asked the Jackal slyly.

'I feel so lonely hunting all by myself. What is the point of being a good hunter, when you do not have a friend to share your food?'

The Jackal's stomach began to rumble when he heard this. 'So, the Lion *does* want to share his food with me after all,' thought the Jackal. He was becoming very hungry simply thinking about all the food he might be able to get from the Lion. And so the Jackal turned to the Lion and said: 'I will be your friend and hunt with you.'

The Lion gave a big smile and said: 'Really? Oh, that makes me very happy indeed!'

Then, pretending to yawn, the Jackal exclaimed: 'But I am so tired from hunting all morning. Perhaps you should go out hunting without me in the meantime. I am going to rest for a while, and then I will join you later.'

The Lion was disappointed at that, but he thought to himself: 'I guess it won't hurt me to go out hunting alone. After all, it will only be for a little while.' The Lion turned to the Jackal and said: 'Very well, Jackal, but do not rest for too long.'

The Jackal replied: 'Do not worry, friend, I will join you soon.' The Jackal gave the Lion a wink and lay back down in the sun.

The Lion set off, feeling very pleased that the Jackal had called him his friend. 'I will never be lonely again,' he said out loud.

As if out of nowhere, the Lion heard a little voice say: 'I would not be so sure of that, if I was you.'

He quickly spun around, 'Who said that?'

Kaggen jumped out from behind a rock and said: 'Listen to me, Lion. Jackal is only trying to trick you.'

The Lion shook his head and said: 'No, Kaggen. Jackal is my friend and we are going hunting together.'

Kaggen folded his arms and looked around. 'Why is he not helping you then?' he asked the Lion.

The Lion looked a bit uncomfortable and mumbled: 'Jackal is resting now, but he is coming to help me very soon.'

Kaggen jumped up onto the rock and said: 'Ha! You see, that clever Jackal is going to make you do all the work.'

But the Lion was too proud and stubborn to listen to Kaggen so he said: 'Out of my way, Kaggen. I have some hunting to do.'

Kaggen threw his arms in the air and cried out: 'I give up! I am not going to warn you again.' And with that, the little mantis disappeared.

After a few hours, the Lion also began to wonder where the Jackal was. 'The Jackal is my friend, I am sure he will be here soon,' he said, trying to convince himself. A few more hours passed, but there was still no sign of the Jackal.

By sunset, the Lion was very tired. He had been hunting alone all day long, and had more than enough meat for both himself and the Jackal. 'I will wait here for Jackal; he is going to be so pleased when he sees how much there is to eat,' thought the Lion as he lay down to rest. The Lion waited and waited. After a little while, he decided that he could not wait any longer and would have to go and look for the Jackal. 'I cannot leave all this food here, someone might come and eat it. I am going to have to take it with me.'

And so the poor Lion set off in search of the Jackal, carrying a very heavy load. In the meantime, the lazy Jackal had only just woken up from his nap. When he saw the Lion coming towards him carrying so much meat, he rubbed his hands together and said: 'Yummy, it looks like dinner time.'

The Lion was panting by the time he reached the Jackal. 'Where have you been?' he asked, trying to catch his breath.

The Jackal answered: 'I am so sorry, my friend. I have only just awoken.'

The Lion was too hungry and tired to be angry, so he said: 'Never mind, we can hunt together tomorrow. Let's eat now.' The Jackal did not waste any time helping himself to the Lion's meat.

The Lion and the Jackal ate their fill, and then saw that there was still plenty of meat left over. The Lion turned to the Jackal and said: 'There is too much meat for us to eat. I think I will go and see if my friend Kaggen wants to share it with us.' The Lion was feeling bad about the way he had treated Kaggen earlier.

But the Jackal did not want to share the meat. 'I must try and find a way to keep all this meat for myself,' he thought. Suddenly, the Jackal had an idea. 'Let's dig a hole to bury the meat in, and then we can look for Kaggen.'

The Lion slapped the Jackal on the back and said: 'That's a fine idea.'

When they had finished digging the hole, the Jackal said to the Lion: 'Maybe you should go and find Kaggen. I will wait here and make sure that no one else finds the meat.'

The Lion thought that the Jackal was being very kind. 'Kaggen will see that he was wrong about Jackal,' the Lion said to himself. He gave the Jackal a big smile and said: 'Good thinking, my friend. See you later!'

As soon as the Jackal could no longer see the Lion, he dug another hole that was further away. Then he dug up all the meat that they had hidden and hid it in the other hole. The Jackal had just finished filling up the first hole with sand when along came the Lion and Kaggen.

As they approached him, the Jackal heard the Lion say to Kaggen: 'I will show you that Jackal is not up to any tricks.'

To this Kaggen answered: 'I do not care what you say, Lion. I do not trust that crafty Jackal.' The Jackal covered his mouth so they would not hear him laugh, and quickly ran off to find somewhere to hide.

The Lion was puzzled when he saw that the Jackal was not there. 'It is strange that Jackal is not here,' he said out loud.

'I warned you. I told you not to trust that Jackal,' Kaggen wagged his finger at the Lion.

But the Lion said: 'Do not be so unkind, Kaggen. I am sure there is a good reason why Jackal is not here.' And then he begun to look for the meat that he and the Jackal had buried earlier. The Lion dug deeper and deeper, but still he could not find the meat.

Kaggen stared down into the hole and said: 'I do not think you are going to find any meat down there.'

The Lion wiped the sweat from his face and said: 'I am sure this is where Jackal and I buried the meat.'

Kaggen began to laugh. 'Jackal has tricked you again!' he cried out.

The Lion realised that Kaggen had been right. The Jackal had him fooled from the start. He had tricked the Lion into doing the hunting all by himself and then, to make matters worse, the Jackal had stolen his meat from right under his nose. The Lion let out a loud roar and disappeared into the night. As he ran off, Kaggen heard him cry out: 'Wait till I get my hands on that Jackal!'

Kaggen shook his head and thought: 'Poor old Lion, I hope he has learnt his lesson.' The Lion certainly did, and from that day on, he always hunted alone.

KAGGEN AND THE ELEPHANT

A story based on the version that appears in The Mantis and his Friends: Bushman Folklore, *D.F. Bleek (1923). Maskew Miller: Cape Town.*

Early one morning, before the sun was high in the sky, Kaggen, the praying mantis, set out with the Walking Stick to find some roots to eat. As he passed by some trees, he heard a voice cry out: 'Oh dear, what ever am I going to do?'

When Kaggen heard the voice, he turned around to see who it was. The Walking Stick knew that Kaggen was always poking his nose where it did not belong, so he said: 'Don't even think about it, Kaggen!'

The Walking Stick did not want to stop; he was hungry and he wanted to find something to eat as soon as possible. But Kaggen was a curious little mantis and said to the Walking Stick: 'We must go and see, maybe we can help.' The Shoes began to giggle when they saw how cross the Walking Stick looked.

'Kaggen is right,' said the Bag in a kind voice, 'maybe someone is in trouble and we can help.'

The Walking Stick threw himself on the ground and, in a loud voice, said: 'Why do I bother?'

Kaggen peered through the trees. 'Sshhh,' he whispered to the Walking Stick, and held up a finger to his lips. Kaggen saw that it was the Springbok, and beside her was little baby Springbok.

Kaggen stepped out from behind the trees and said: 'Hello Springbok. My friends and I were passing by and we thought you were having some trouble.'

The Springbok jumped into the air: 'It's only you, Kaggen. You gave me such a fright.' And then she smiled and said: 'What a sweet little mantis you are. I am not in trouble, but I do have a problem.'

Kaggen bowed low in front of the Springbok and said: 'Maybe I can be of help?'

The Walking Stick started to sulk and said: 'Oh boy, here we go again. It is going to be hours before we eat.'

The Springbok shook her head and answered: 'Thank you, Kaggen, that is very kind of you, but you will not be able to help me unless you know someone who can look after my baby for a little while.'

Kaggen gave a big smile and said: 'But I do know someone ... me!'

The Springbok laughed: 'You, Kaggen?'

Kaggen puffed out his chest and said: 'Well, why not?'

The Springbok patted Kaggen on the head. 'Because you are always up to mischief,' replied the Springbok.

When the Bag saw how hurt Kaggen looked, he said to the Springbok: 'Kaggen will not be on his own; we can also help.'

The Springbok became quiet and, after thinking about it for a moment, she said: 'All right, I will let you look after baby Springbok.'

Kaggen was so pleased that he jumped up and kicked his heels together. The Springbok said goodbye to her little one and, just before she ran off, she said: 'Whatever you do, keep an eye on baby Springbok all the time.'

Kaggen waved and shouted out after her: 'Do not worry, I will take good care of her!'

When the Springbok was out of sight, the Walking Stick pointed at the baby Springbok and said: 'What are we going to do with her?'

Kaggen grinned and said: 'Well, she can come with us to look for roots, of course.'

And with that, they all set off together. This looks like a good place to dig,' said Kaggen, after they had been walking for a little while. They were all very hungry, and their stomachs had started to rumble. Kaggen turned to his things and said: 'You keep an eye on baby Springbok while I dig.'

And so Kaggen began to dig. He dug for a little while, but he did not find any roots. The hole became deeper and deeper, but still he did not find anything. Kaggen was so busy digging that he did not see that, one by one, the Bag, the Walking Stick and the Shoes had all fallen asleep in the warm sun.

When, at last, Kaggen found some roots, he had dug so deep that he could not even see out of the hole. 'Hey, everybody! We can eat now!' he called from inside the hole. But no one answered him. Kaggen thought this was very strange, so he climbed out of the hole. To his dismay, he found all his things fast asleep and baby Springbok nowhere in sight! 'Wake up! Wake up! Where is baby Springbok?' yelled Kaggen in such a loud voice that the Shoes woke up with a jump.

The Bag gave a big yawn and said: 'What do you mean? She is here.'

Kaggen stamped his foot and shouted: 'No, she is not!'

When they realised that baby Springbok was nowhere to be seen, the Shoes cried out: 'Oh no, we've lost her!'

Kaggen sat down with his head in his hands and said: 'What am I going to tell Springbok?'

The Walking Stick tapped hard on the ground and said: 'I knew this was a bad idea from the start.'

Kaggen looked at the Walking Stick, who was looking very smug. Just then, he saw a big footprint. 'Look at this,' he called to his things.

'And there are more over here!' said the Shoes excitedly.

The Bag looked down and took a closer look. He said: 'These footprints belong to Elephant.'

The Shoes began to cry. 'Elephant has taken baby Springbok away and it is all our fault,' they sobbed between their tears.

Kaggen patted the Shoes and said: 'Do not cry, little friends. I will think of a plan to rescue baby Springbok, but first we must tell Springbok what has happened.' And so off they went.

As Kaggen neared the trees where they had first met the Springbok, they saw her running towards them. From a distance, the Springbok saw their long faces and knew something was wrong: 'Where is my baby?' she asked, looking around.

Kaggen looked away and, in a small voice, he said: 'Elephant has taken baby Springbok.'

Wide-eyed, the Springbok stared at Kaggen and said: 'I told you not let her out of your sight! How did it happen?'

Kaggen felt so guilty that he could not even look at the Springbok. 'I was inside a hole and did not see Elephant,' he said, with his head down low.

'You naughty mantis. If you did not hear or see Elephant, then you must have been asleep,' she scolded.

Kaggen looked at the Springbok for the first time and said: 'Please do not be angry. I promise I will bring baby Springbok back from Elephant.' Then Kaggen called to his things and said: 'Come along! We are going to follow those footprints and find baby Springbok.'

As the Springbok watched them go, she called out: 'Do not come back until you have my baby.'

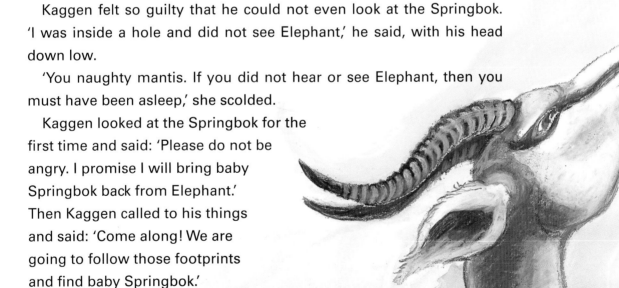

Kaggen turned back to the place where he had been digging the hole and followed the footprints until he reached a big field. 'I think I see Elephant,' Kaggen said, shading his eyes from the sun. Then he had an idea. 'You take a closer look and tell me if you can see if Elephant has baby Springbok,' he said to the Shoes.

'You can count on us,' they answered and ran off. After a few minutes, the Shoes came running back, looking very excited: 'We saw her! We saw baby Springbok!'

Kaggen clapped his hands together and said: 'Well done, Shoes!' And then he added: 'Tell me more. What else did you see?'

The Shoes had been running so fast that they had to stop and catch their breath before they could tell Kaggen anything more. But Kaggen could not wait any longer, and before the Shoes could say anything, off he went to see for himself. As he approached the field, Kaggen saw the Elephant. He was watching over baby Elephant and baby Springbok as they played together.

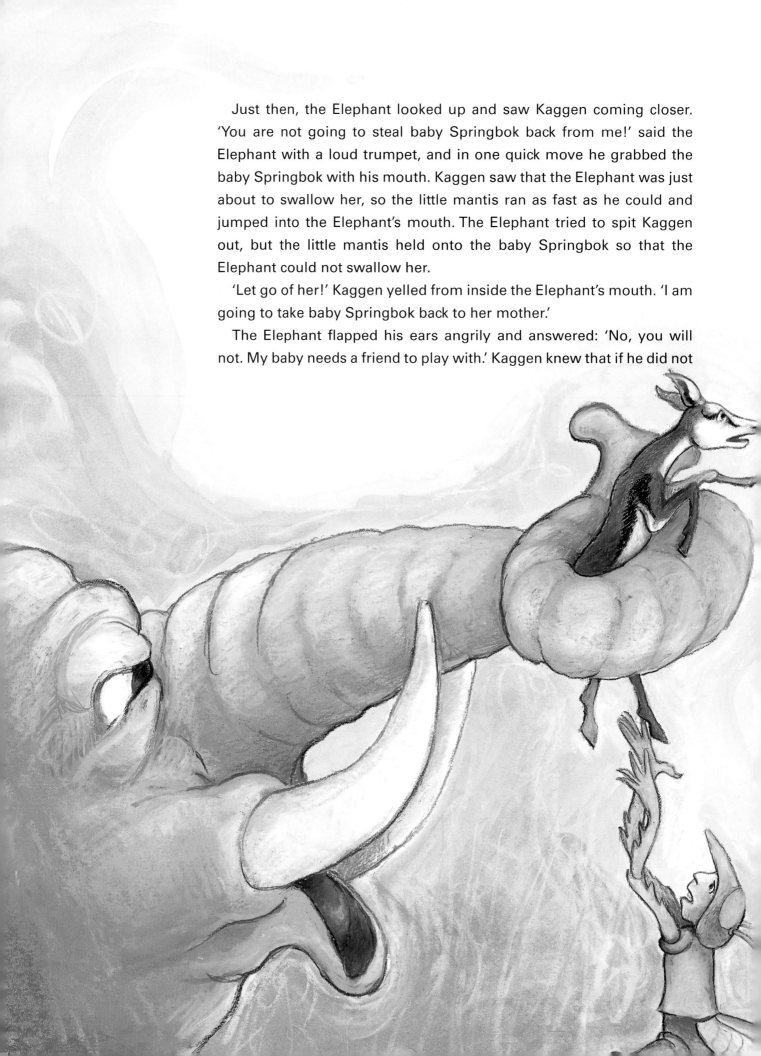

Just then, the Elephant looked up and saw Kaggen coming closer. 'You are not going to steal baby Springbok back from me!' said the Elephant with a loud trumpet, and in one quick move he grabbed the baby Springbok with his mouth. Kaggen saw that the Elephant was just about to swallow her, so the little mantis ran as fast as he could and jumped into the Elephant's mouth. The Elephant tried to spit Kaggen out, but the little mantis held onto the baby Springbok so that the Elephant could not swallow her.

'Let go of her!' Kaggen yelled from inside the Elephant's mouth. 'I am going to take baby Springbok back to her mother.'

The Elephant flapped his ears angrily and answered: 'No, you will not. My baby needs a friend to play with.' Kaggen knew that if he did not do something soon, he and the baby Springbok would both be swallowed. Then Kaggen thought of something very clever. He began to tickle the Elephant's throat.

'Stop that!' the Elephant cried out, coughing. But Kaggen tickled and tickled until the Elephant coughed so hard that he spat out both Kaggen and the baby Springbok! Kaggen quickly grabbed the baby Springbok and, to the Elephant's great surprise, the mantis grew feathers and flew off immediately.

The Walking Stick, the Shoes and the Bag gave a big cheer when they saw Kaggen flying towards them with the baby Springbok in his arms: 'Hooray! Kaggen's done it! Hooray! Kaggen has saved baby Springbok!' The poor baby Springbok was so scared to have almost been swallowed by the Elephant that she was still shaking.

'Do not worry, baby Springbok. You will soon be home, safe and sound,' Kaggen said, as he gently put her down on the ground. The Bag saw that the sun was about to set, and said: 'We had better be going if we want to get this little one home before dark.'

Kaggen stroked the baby Springbok and said: 'Come along, then. I think we have all had enough adventure for one day.'

The Walking Stick tapped Kaggen lightly on the head: '*You* can never have enough adventure, Kaggen.'

This made everyone laugh and, singing all the way, they set off to find the Springbok. When the Springbok saw them coming, she was so happy that they had found baby Springbok that she ran up to meet them. 'I promise to never leave you again,' she said to the baby Springbok, licking her all over.

The Springbok kept her promise and that is why today, if you ever see the Springbok, her baby is always close by and never leaves her side.

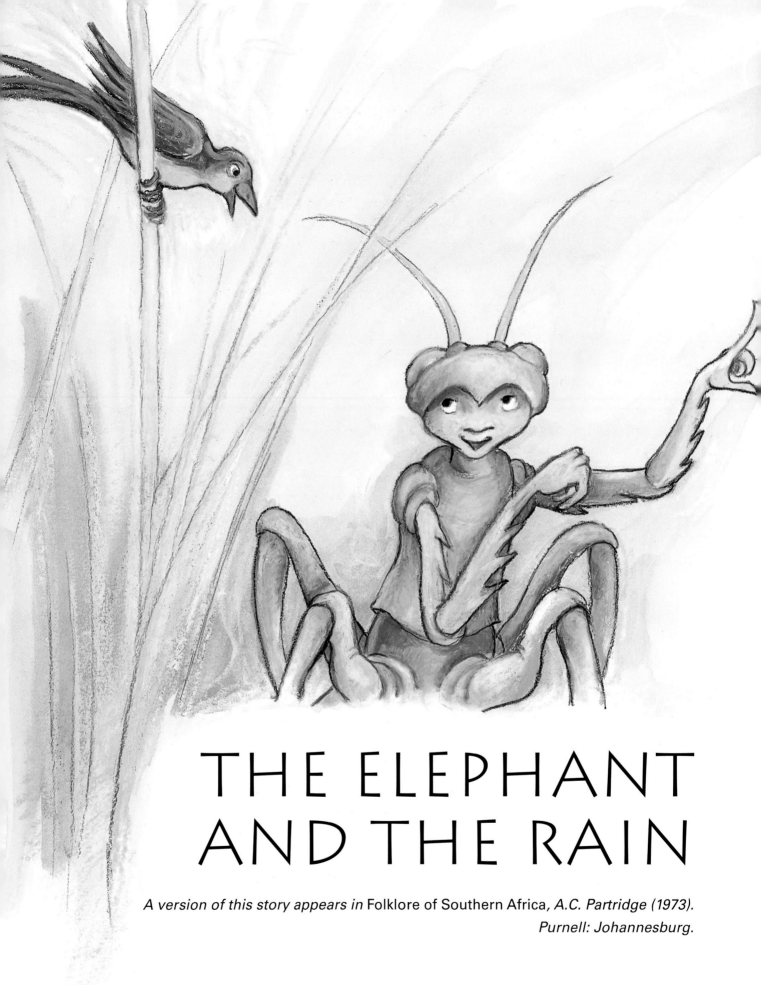

THE ELEPHANT
AND THE RAIN

A version of this story appears in Folklore of Southern Africa, *A.C. Partridge (1973).*
Purnell: Johannesburg.

One hot and dry day, Kaggen was lying under the shade of a tree. Just then, the Bush-Bird flew by, carrying a string of white beads. 'Hello, Bush-Bird, you look as though you are in a hurry,' said Kaggen.

'I certainly am!' replied the Bush-Bird, out of breath. 'I am delivering a message from Elephant to his wife, Rain. She has run away to her family in the clouds because she is angry with him. She refuses to return to Elephant, so now there is almost no water left in the waterhole and we are becoming more and more thirsty.'

'No wonder it is so hot!' exclaimed Kaggen. 'Why do you not rest for a minute and tell me what Elephant did to make his wife, Rain, quite so angry? Maybe I can help you persuade Rain to return to Elephant?' suggested Kaggen.

'I do not know if that is such a good idea,' said the Bush-Bird nervously, 'I really cannot waste any more time.'

'Very well then, but let me come with you to find Rain and, on the way, you can tell me why she is angry with Elephant,' said Kaggen, who would never take 'no' for an answer.

By now the Bush-Bird was so impatient to go that she would have agreed to anything. She let out an exasperated sigh, threw up her little wings and said: 'I give up, Kaggen, you win! But can we please move on?' And with that, Bush-Bird flew off, with Kaggen and his belongings hot on her trail.

'I am going to need my wings to keep up with Bush-Bird. She may be small, but she sure is fast!' exclaimed Kaggen.

The Shoes were panting as they tried to keep up with Kaggen and could have jumped for joy when they heard Kaggen was going to use his wings.

'Hooray!' they cheered as he put the Shoes on his feet and slung the Bag across his back.

'Hold on tight!' he warned. The Walking Stick jumped into Kaggen's hand just in time as they began to fly, soaring higher and higher into the sky until they could see the Bush-Bird just ahead of them.

'There you are, Kaggen. I thought you would have given up by now. You really are a determined little mantis,' teased the Bush-Bird.

As they flew higher and closer to the clouds in search of the Rain, the Bush-Bird told Kaggen why the Rain had run away from her husband, the Elephant.

The Elephant and the Rain were happily married until, one day, the Elephant asked her: 'Rain, who do you really think is the strongest in the land?'

The Rain did not think it mattered who was the strongest. She said to the Elephant: 'I think everyone is strong in their own way.'

This was not what the Elephant wanted to hear. In a loud, booming voice he said: 'I am the mighty Elephant, and I am the strongest in the land.' The Rain was startled by the Elephant's loud voice, but she did not say anything. 'Did you not hear me, Rain?' asked the Elephant. 'I am the mighty Elephant, and I am the strongest in the land,' he said again, this time even louder.

After some time Rain said in a soft but clear voice: 'You may be strong, my husband, but I am Rain. I bring water for all the animals when they are thirsty. I water all the plants and trees so that they can grow.'

But this was still not what the Elephant wanted to hear. The Rain's words made the Elephant angry. He stamped his foot and flapped his big ears, causing everything to tremble around him. He said again, even louder this time: 'I am the mighty Elephant, and I am strongest in the land.'

The Rain was not afraid of the Elephant. She just smiled and said again: 'You may be strong, my husband, but I am Rain. I bring water for all the animals when they are thirsty. I water all the plants and trees so that they can grow.'

The Elephant grew even angrier when he saw that Rain was not afraid of him. He took a deep breath and trumpeted loudly, as loudly as he could. Then he wrapped his trunk around the biggest tree he could find and pulled it out of the ground. The Rain looked at the uprooted tree, but she did not say anything. The Elephant saw that the Rain was shaking.

He said to himself: 'Aha! Now she can see for herself how strong I am. I think my wife is beginning to be afraid of me.'

The Elephant trumpeted loudly once again. This time it was to call all the animals in the land so that he could show them how his strength had silenced his wife and made her tremble in fear. The Rain was quiet and trembling not because she was afraid, but because she was angry and deep in thought. The Rain stared at the uprooted tree for a long time, wondering whether she should stab her husband with her tongue of lightning.

Meanwhile, the longer she remained quiet, the more nervous the Elephant began to feel. 'Why does she not *say* anything? Why does she not *do* anything?' he thought angrily to himself. But the Rain said nothing. She thought and thought, never taking her eyes off the uprooted tree. Eventually she saw that the tree had started to die and the leaves were drying and falling off. This gave Rain an idea.

Meanwhile, all the other animals in the land had heard the Elephant's call and began to make their way to where the Elephant and the Rain were. The Ostrich was the first to arrive. Her long legs helped her to run very fast! Right behind the Ostrich was the Giraffe. He was in such a hurry to see what all the noise was about that he had stretched his long neck out as far as he could. Then along came the Zebra, the Springbok and the Crane. Even the proud Lion and the shy old Tortoise had come to see what all the fuss was about.

Once all the animals had gathered around the Elephant, the Rain spoke to her husband for the first time in a strong voice for all to hear: 'Your pride and your boasting will cause you to wither and die of thirst, just like the leaves of this great tree which you destroyed. I am leaving you to return to my family in the clouds.'

These words scared the Elephant, but he was too proud to let the other animals see how afraid he was. And so he replied: 'Go! I do not need you. I will find all the water I need without your help.'

When the Elephant said those words, the Rain took the rainbow she always wore around her waist, waved it over the land and disappeared.

Then the strangest thing began to happen. As soon as the Rain disappeared, the land became dry and hard. All the animals looked around in horror. They cried out to the Elephant: 'What have you done, you proud old fool? You have made Rain angry, and she has gone back to her family in the clouds. Now there is nothing for us to drink. We will all die of thirst because of you!'

But the stubborn Elephant would not listen and told all the animals to go home. After a few hours the Elephant began to feel hungry, and went in search of something to eat. He found a big tree and began to chew the bark. To his horror, the bark was not sweet and sticky as it usually was. Instead, the bark was dry and hard. 'Phew!' said the Elephant and spat out the dry bark in disgust. He then went to the

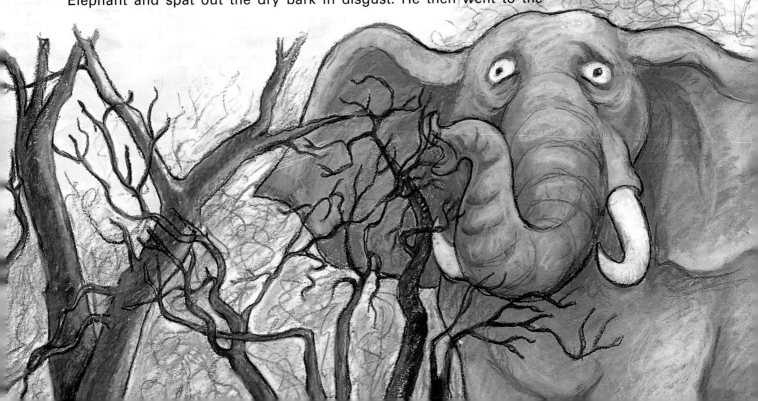

swamp in search of food, but when he reached it, he found that the swamp was not sticky and wet. It had become dry, hard ground.

The Elephant became hungrier and hungrier. As he looked for food, his throat became drier and drier. As the air became hotter and drier, the most curious thing began to happen to the Elephant. He began to shrink. Soon, the Elephant became very tired, and decided to rest under the shade of a tree. After some time, he heard the whistle of the Bush-Bird.

The Elephant called out to the Bush-Bird in a weak voice: 'Bush-Bird, I need your help. I have made Rain angry, so she has run away to her family in the clouds. Tell her than I am shrinking. I need her to come back or I will die of thirst. Take this string of white beads from around my neck so she will know that I sent you.'

The Bush-Bird let out a long whistle when she saw how the strong Elephant had become too small and weak to even stand up. She flew off in search of the Rain as fast as her little wings could carry her.

Kaggen was listening so carefully to the Bush-Bird's story that he did not notice that they had become completely surrounded by clouds. 'Look at all these clouds!' exclaimed the Shoes.

The Bush-Bird said: 'Rain must be somewhere close by.'

Just then, they heard a soft, but clear voice: 'Who are you, and why are you looking for Rain?'

They all looked around, but there was nobody there apart from themselves. Kaggen cleared his throat and replied: 'I am Kaggen, the mantis, and this is Bush-Bird. We have been sent to find Rain. We have a message from her husband, Elephant.'

'Why should I believe you?' answered the voice.

'Look, Bush-Bird has the necklace that Rain gave Elephant. He gave it to us to prove that he sent us. Please, you must tell us where we can find Rain,' pleaded Kaggen.

And suddenly she appeared, wrapped in a dark blanket and the air filled with the smell of Rain: 'I do not want to hear any messages from that stubborn old fool.'

'But Elephant wants you to come back,' said Kaggen.

'I will never go back!' said the Rain, her voice becoming louder.

'You do not understand,' wailed the Bush-Bird, 'your husband is shrinking. He is dying of thirst.'

The Bush-Bird's words made the Rain quiet. She was angry at the Elephant for being so boastful and stubborn, but she still cared for him and did not want him to die of thirst. The Rain let out a big sigh and said: 'Very well, Bush-Bird. I will go and help my husband, but I hope that he has learnt his lesson.'

And with those words, the Rain went to look for the Elephant. When she finally found him, he had shrunk so much that he looked like a dry leaf lying under a tree. When the Elephant saw the Rain coming, he had just enough strength to open his mouth and fill himself with water. After the Rain had returned to live with her husband in the veld, it was not long before the Elephant was back to his old self, but it was said that he was never heard boasting again.

KAGGEN TRICKS THE WORKER BEES

Based on the collection, Bushman Stories, *E.W. Thomas (1950). Oxford University Press: Cape Town, London and New York.*

One morning, Kaggen woke up and saw it was a bright and sunny day. 'Hooray!' he yelled as he jumped out of bed. It had been raining for days, and the poor little mantis had been so bored. It was hard to be up to mischief when you were stuck inside all day!

'I wonder what I should do today,' thought Kaggen, as he yawned and stretched his legs in the morning sun. Just then, his stomach let out a loud rumble. This gave him an idea. 'I think I will go and visit the Worker Bees. They make the most delicious honey, and I am sure they will give me some if I tell them how hungry I am.' Feeling pleased with his plan, Kaggen wasted no more time and set off in search of their beehive.

It was not long before Kaggen began to hear a soft hum in the distance. 'That sounds like the Worker Bees; I must be close,' thought Kaggen, rubbing his stomach. His stomach answered with another noisy rumble. He was becoming hungrier by the minute and began to walk faster.

With every step he took, he could hear the humming growing louder and louder: 'Buzzzzz! BUZZZZZ!' Suddenly, Kaggen could hear that the humming noise was very close. In fact, it was coming from right inside his own ear! Kaggen shook his head furiously, and out popped a little Worker Bee.

'Oops,' squealed the Worker Bee. 'Sorry, I was in such a hurry that I did not look where I was going. Before I knew it, I had flown right into your ear,' he explained in a little voice.

'Do not worry about that, my little friend,' replied Kaggen, scratching his ear. 'But before you go, I have a favour to ask you.' Then, in his most polite voice, Kaggen said: 'I am so very hungry, Worker Bee, could you please give me some honey?'

'Phew,' answered the Worker Bee, wiping his forehead, 'I have been working all day and the Queen Bee will be furious if she knows that I have given you some of her honey.'

Kaggen looked so disappointed that the Bee felt sorry for him and said: 'Oh, all right, I suppose it will not do any harm to give you a little bit of honey. Come along then, Kaggen, you can follow me to the hive.' And off they went.

When they arrived there, Kaggen could not believe his eyes. Hundreds of little Worker Bees were flying in and out of the hive. His mouth began to water just thinking about all that sweet honey inside.

'Help yourself, Kaggen,' said the Bee, 'but remember, not too much.'

Kaggen stuck his hand into the hive and grabbed a handful of honey. 'Thank you, little Bee,' said Kaggen, gulping down the honey. Honey was Kaggen's favourite food and, being such a greedy mantis, that little bit was not nearly enough for him. 'I need to find a way of getting some more honey,' said Kaggen to himself.

He was thinking so hard that he hardly heard the Bee say to him: 'Goodbye. I must go back to work now. Have a good journey.'

Kaggen began to grin: 'That's it, a journey!' The Bee had given him a good idea. Quickly he called out to the Bee: 'There is one more thing, little Bee. I am on a journey with a friend who will be coming along a bit later. Do you mind giving him some honey, too?'

By this time, the Bee was in a great hurry to go back to his work and said: 'Very well, but your friend cannot have too much honey either.'

Before Kaggen had a chance to thank him, the Bee disappeared into the hive. Kaggen rubbed his hands together and thought to himself: 'I will go and nap in the shade and then, after a little while, I will go and trick the Bees into thinking that I am someone else.'

After a few hours, Kaggen woke up from his nap. He was hungry again, and ready to eat more honey. 'First I must find a way to disguise myself,' said Kaggen, scratching his head. Suddenly, he saw the Hare pass by. 'Hello there, Hare!' shouted Kaggen.

The Hare stopped and turned around: 'What do you want, Kaggen?'

'Come closer Hare, I need your help,' yelled Kaggen.

The Hare, knowing that Kaggen was always up to mischief, shook his head:

'Sorry Kaggen, I am not going to fall for any of your tricks.'

Kaggen pretended to howl in pain: 'Oh, please help me, Hare. The Bees stung me on my head when I tried to take some of their honey.'

The Hare began to chuckle: 'Ha! Ha! Serves you right, Kaggen.'

Kaggen howled even louder: 'Oh, my poor head. Please, Hare, come closer, so I can show you where the Bees stung me.'

'Poor Kaggen,' thought the Hare, 'his head must be very sore. I will have a look and see if I can help him.'

As the Hare came close to Kaggen, Kaggen reached out and grabbed some fur off the Hare's back!

'Ouch!' yelled the Hare and tried to grab Kaggen, but he had vanished in a cloud of dust. Shaking his fist in the air, the Hare shouted: 'You cheeky mantis! One day you will be sorry for all the trouble you cause.'

But Kaggen was long gone and did not hear the Hare's angry words. When Kaggen was sure that he was far enough away from the Hare, he sat down on a nearby rock. 'Now that I have some of the Hare's fur, I can make myself a wig. The Bees will never guess that it is me asking for honey,' said Kaggen, laughing to himself.

When Kaggen had finished making the wig, he made his way back to the hive. The Bees were as busy as ever.

'Excuse me,' he called out to one of the Worker Bees as they zoomed past him. 'I am so hungry and tired. My friend Kaggen is way ahead of me. Do you think you could give me some honey?'

The Worker Bee said: 'Yes, yes, Kaggen told us you were coming, and that you would want some honey. But do hurry up! We are very busy, as you can see.'

Once again, Kaggen stuck his hand into the hive and grabbed a handful of honey. As soon as Kaggen had gulped down the honey he said to the Bee: 'Thanks, you have been so kind. I have a friend who is a little way behind me and I am sure he will also be very hungry. Can you give him a little bit of your honey, too?'

The Worker Bee rolled his eyes: 'What? Not another friend wanting some of our honey!' Before Kaggen could say anything more, he added: 'Oh, very well. I do not have time to talk this over with you anyway, I must be off.'

And, on hearing those words, Kaggen skipped off and began pulling off his wig as he sang:

'I tricked the Bees! I tricked the Bees!
They've given me their honey.
Isn't that funny? Isn't that funny?

I tricked the Bees! I tricked the Bees!
They've given me their honey.
Isn't that funny? Isn't that funny?'

Kaggen was so busy singing to himself that he did not see that one Worker Bee had flown past him and overheard his song. The Bee rushed back to the hive to tell the others that Kaggen had used a wig to disguise himself. Soon all the Worker Bees knew that Kaggen had tricked them, and gathered together to decide what to do.

'Someone has to tell the Queen,' one of them cried out.

'But who will it be?' said another.

'Which one of us told Kaggen he could have some honey in the first place?' asked a Worker Bee. Suddenly all the Bees went quiet.

'Ahem,' said a little voice, 'it was me.' All the Bees turned around and there stood the Bee that had flown into Kaggen's ear. 'I will have to tell the Queen,' he said, trying not to look at all the angry faces of the other Bees. And with that, the poor little Bee flew off to find the Queen. He flew deeper and deeper into the warm, sticky hive. As he came closer to the Queen's rooms, he heard a loud snore. 'Oh no,' thought the Bee to himself, 'I will have to wake her up. She's going to be even more angry with me.'

He gave a quiet little knock on her door and flew in. The Queen was indeed fast asleep. Her mouth was wide open, and she was snoring.

'I am so sorry to wake you, my dear Queen,' whispered the Bee. But the Queen simply let out a grunt and rolled over. The Bee tried again and, this time, in a louder voice he said: 'I am so sorry to wake you, my dear Queen.'

The Queen Bee woke up and began to rub her eyes. The little Bee trembled with fear. The Queen sat up and, wiping some dried honey from her mouth, she said irritably: 'What do you want? Why aren't you working?'

The little Bee looked up at the Queen and said: 'I g-g-gave K-K-Kaggen some h-h-h-honey.' He was so scared he could hardly speak.

When the Queen heard that Kaggen had eaten her honey, she screamed so loudly that all the Bees in the hive had to cover their ears. 'How dare he steal from me,' she roared, 'don't you dare let that trickster near my honey again!'

In the meantime, Kaggen had used the Hare's fur to make a beard for himself. As he made his way back to the hive, he could not stop thinking about all that delicious honey. 'Maybe this time I should try to take a bigger handful,' he said out loud. When he arrived at the hive, Kaggen called out in a deep voice: 'Hello, Bees, I have been travelling for so long – do you have some honey for me?'

But the Bees knew better, and could not be fooled again: 'No Kaggen, we know what you have been up to, and the Queen is furious.'

When he saw that his deception had been discovered, Kaggen's face turned a deep shade of red. 'But I am not Kaggen,' he said to the Bees and tried to reach into the hive to grab the honey. But the Bees were too fast for him.

Suddenly hundreds of Bees flew out of the hive and began to pull off his beard. 'We know it's you, Kaggen,' they cried out.

'Ouch!' yelled Kaggen as some of the Bees began to sting him. 'Ouch! Stop that, it hurts!' Kaggen tried to cover his head with his hands but the Bees would not leave him alone. They were very angry that Kaggen had tricked them and stolen their honey! Poor Kaggen, all that was left for him to do was run away as fast as he could.

The Worker Bees cheered as they watched Kaggen run off, holding his head and howling in pain. That was the last they ever saw of the mischievous mantis because, from that day on, Kaggen never tried to steal honey from the Worker Bees again.

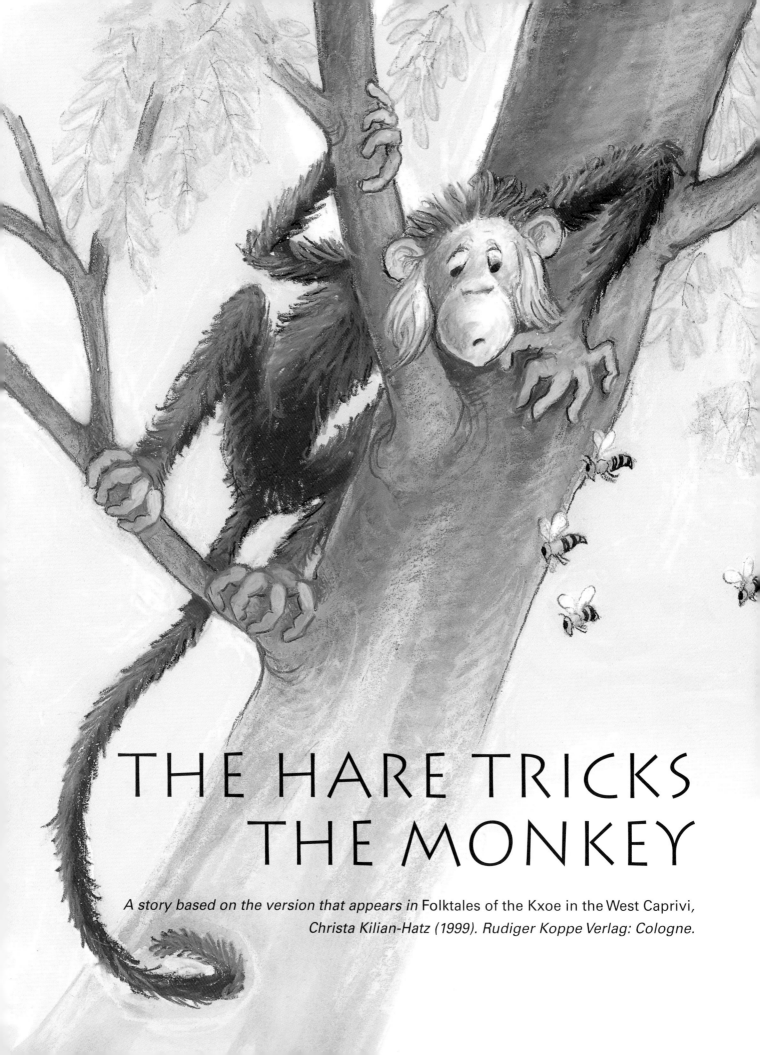

THE HARE TRICKS THE MONKEY

A story based on the version that appears in Folktales of the Kxoe in the West Caprivi, *Christa Kilian-Hatz (1999). Rudiger Koppe Verlag: Cologne.*

One afternoon, the Monkey was hanging upside down in a tree. As he swayed from side to side, he spotted a beehive. This gave the naughty Monkey an idea. He swung from one branch to another until he was right above the beehive. And then, using his feet, he quickly scooped some honey out of the hive.

The Bees buzzed angrily after him: 'You cheeky Monkey! Leave our honey alone or we will sting you.'

But the Monkey did not care about the angry Bees and just laughed. 'You will have to catch me first!' he said, as he disappeared into the trees. When he had found a safe place, the Monkey began to eat the honey. Just then he saw the Hare walking by, so he called out: 'Hello there, Hare.'

The Hare looked up and said: 'Oh, it's you, Monkey. Hello. What are you up to?'

The Monkey flashed a cheeky grin and said: 'I stole some honey from the Bees and it is delicious. Wouldn't you like to come up and share it with me?'

The Hare replied: 'You know very well that I cannot climb trees, why do you not come down here instead?'

But the Monkey gave the Hare another cheeky grin and said: 'Come on, Hare. It is easy to climb up here!'

The Hare was becoming angry with the Monkey: 'Stop teasing me, you know that I can only run on flat ground and over rocks or bushes.'

The Monkey laughed at the Hare and said: 'All right, Hare. I can see you are too scared to climb up here so I will come down to you.'

By this time, the Hare was very angry at the Monkey for teasing him, but he also wanted some of the honey so he did not say anything back. The Monkey swung down from the tree until he was almost on the ground. Then he opened his hand and said: 'Here you go, my friend. Help yourself.'

But when the Hare reached up to take some honey, he saw that the Monkey's hand was empty. 'I will catch you, naughty Monkey! First you tease me and now you fool me into thinking you are going to share your honey with me!' shouted the Hare.

But it was too late. The Monkey had already climbed high up into the tree, and was pointing and laughing at the angry Hare. Fuming, the Hare hopped away.

When he arrived home, the Hare thought to himself: 'Monkey is always playing tricks on others, I think it is time that someone played a trick on him.'

He lay awake all night, until he had come up with a plan to pay the Monkey back. By sunrise, the Hare had an idea, but he would need some help. Later that morning, the Hare went off in search of the Bees. As the Hare neared the beehive, a swarm of Bees came flying out of the hive towards him. The Hare called out: 'Wait! Do not sting me. I have not come to steal your honey.'

The Bees flew right up to the Hare until they nearly touched his nose. 'So, why are you here?' they buzzed loudly.

The Hare stood very still and replied: 'I want to play a trick on Monkey, and I need your help.'

When they heard this, the Bees stopped their buzzing and began to whisper very softly among themselves. The Hare tried to listen with his long ears, but he could not hear what they were saying.

Finally, one of the Bees turned around to look at the Hare and said: 'Very well, Hare. We will help you. We also want to punish Monkey for stealing our honey.'

The Hare rubbed his hands together and said to the Bee: 'Great! Now, all I need from you is some of your delicious honey.'

70

'Not so fast, my friend,' said the little Bee holding up his hand, 'I need to discuss it with the rest of the Bees first.'

Once again, the Bees huddled together and began whispering to one another. The Hare leaned closer to the Bees, but still he could not hear anything they were saying. Suddenly, they stopped whispering and, without another word, they flew off.

'Wait! Wait! Where are you going? What about my honey?' the Hare called out after them. But the Bees were long gone, and there was nothing else for the poor Hare to do but go home.

'Oh no! What am I going to do now?' thought the Hare to himself as he made his way back to his house. But what the Hare did not know was that there was a surprise waiting for him at home. He could not believe what he saw. He rubbed his eyes and looked again. Sure enough, there was a big pot of honey right on his doorstep!

'Yippee!' cried out the Hare, hopping up and down. He was very excited! The Hare could not wait any longer to play his trick on the Monkey, so off he went to find him.

When the Hare arrived at the tree where the Monkey lived he could not see him, so he looked up and said in a loud voice: 'Hello, Monkey. Are you up there?' The Hare felt someone tap him from behind, but when he turned around, there was no one there. Again he called out: 'Hello, Monkey. Are you up there?' And once again he felt someone tap him, but he could not see anyone. Then he heard a giggle. The Hare looked around and said: 'Who's there? I am looking for Monkey. I want him to come to my house to eat some honey.'

With that the Monkey was hanging upside down, right in front of the Hare. 'Honey!' cried out the Monkey. 'Why did you not say so in the first place?' And then he threw his arm around the Hare and added: 'Well, what are we waiting for?'

The Hare put on his best smile and said: 'You must first give me some time to clean my house before you come and visit.' The Monkey patted the Hare on the back and said: 'All right, but do not be too long. I cannot wait to start on that honey.'

The Hare said goodbye, and rushed back home. Once there, he set fire to the grass outside his house until the ground in front of the house was covered in ash. From a distance, the Bees watched him. 'Whatever could he be up to?' they asked one another. They thought he had gone mad!

After a little while, they saw the Monkey approaching, gleefully rubbing his stomach. The Monkey was so busy thinking about all the delicious honey he was going to eat that he did not even notice that he had walked over all the ash in front of the Hare's house. When the Monkey was right outside the house, he called out to the Hare: 'Yoo-hoo! It is me, Monkey!'

The Hare answered from inside the house: 'Come in, my friend.' The Monkey stepped inside and found the Hare sitting next to a big pot of honey. When he saw how much honey there was, the Monkey's mouth began to water.

The Hare said to him: 'Hold out your hand so that I can give you some honey.' But as the Monkey held out his hand, the Hare cried out: 'Look how dirty you are! You are going to make a mess in my clean house.'

The Monkey looked down at his hands and feet and saw that the Hare was right. 'I cannot let you eat any honey until you are clean. Go and wash in the river and I will start eating this delicious honey,' said the Hare between mouthfuls of honey.

The Monkey was very puzzled. 'How did I become so dirty?' he wondered as he made his way to the river. The Bees watched the Monkey go to the river and wash himself. On his way back, they giggled when they saw that the Monkey was so deep in thought that, once again, he did not see that he had walked in the ash.

When the Monkey returned to the house, he sat down next to the Hare and said: 'Right! Now I'm ready for some honey.'

But when the Monkey held out his hand once more, the Hare said: 'Look, you are still dirty! Go and wash in the river.'

The Monkey looked down at himself and saw how black his hands and feet were. He scratched his head and said: 'I do not understand why I am so dirty when I have just been to wash in the river.'

The Hare just shook his head and said: 'Sorry Monkey, you cannot have any honey until you clean yourself.'

72

The Monkey watched the Hare as he ate the honey, and saw that it was almost finished. 'I'd better hurry, or Hare will finish all that honey!' he thought to himself, and rushed out. On his way back from the river, the Monkey was in such a hurry that, once again, he did not see the ash. He burst through the door and found the Hare was licking the bottom of the honey pot.

'Please leave me that little bit of honey,' begged the Monkey.

The Hare gave a sly smile and said: 'Of course, help yourself.' But when the Monkey reached out for the pot of honey, he saw that the Hare had indeed finished all of it.

The Monkey threw the pot hard on the ground so that it broke into pieces. 'You greedy Hare!' he yelled out to the Hare, who was rolling around on the floor in laughter.

Just then, there was a loud buzzing noise and the Bees swarmed into the house.

'What are you doing with our honey, Monkey?' they asked as they buzzed around the Monkey's head.

'*He* stole your honey,' said the Monkey, pointing to the Hare. But the Bees simply kept flying around and around the Monkey's head and said: 'We warned you that we were going to sting you the next time you stole our honey.'

The Monkey tried to run away but the Bees flew after him. 'Please, Hare. Tell the Bees that I did not steal their honey this time!' the Monkey cried out, as he ran out the door holding his head.

But the Hare just laughed and laughed as he watched the Bees chase the Monkey all the way down to the river. When the Monkey reached the river, the only way he could escape from the Bees was to jump in. And so he did. The Monkey looked so silly trying to swim that it made the Hare cry with laughter.

'I hope you learnt your lesson, Monkey!' the Hare shouted after him, wiping the tears from his eyes. The poor Monkey was too scared to leave the river, and had to wait until the Bees finally left him alone. It was cold and dark by the time it was safe for the Monkey to climb out, all wet and shivering. After that day, it was a long time before the Monkey dared to make any mischief again.

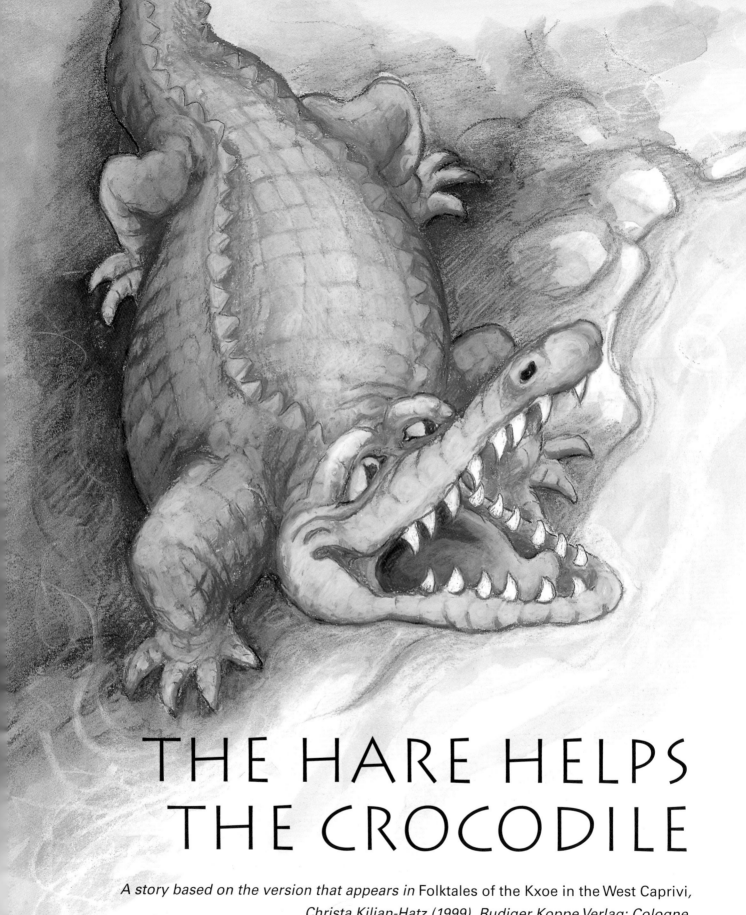

THE HARE HELPS THE CROCODILE

A story based on the version that appears in Folktales of the Kxoe in the West Caprivi, *Christa Kilian-Hatz (1999). Rudiger Koppe Verlag: Cologne.*

One bright and sunny day the old Crocodile was warming his back in the sun. Suddenly, he heard laughing down at the river. He was very curious, and wanted to see who it was. The Crocodile lived in the river all alone, and he did not have visitors very often. Slowly and quietly he crept into the river, and swum closer to have a better look. There he saw the Zebra and the Eland laughing and splashing together in the river. This made the Crocodile feel very sad and lonely.

'Zebra and Eland are having so much fun together. I wish I also had a friend,' thought the Crocodile to himself. The Crocodile watched the Zebra and the Eland play together for a long time. The longer he watched them, the lonelier he felt. 'Soon they will leave the river to go back to the bush, and I will be all alone again,' he thought sadly. This gave the Crocodile an idea. 'Maybe I can go with them!' he said out loud. This idea made the Crocodile happier then he had been in a very long time. He swam right up to where the Zebra and the Eland were splashing about in the water.

When they saw the Crocodile swimming towards them, the Zebra and Eland both let out a shriek.

'Please, do not be afraid. I do not want to eat you,' said the Crocodile in a friendly voice. 'I am tired of living in the river all alone, I would like to follow you to the bush.'

The Eland and the Zebra both began to laugh. 'You silly old fool! We live far away from the river, you will never be able to follow us all the way to the bush,' explained the Zebra.

The Crocodile felt very hurt when he heard the Zebra's words and replied: 'I may be slower, but I can walk just as far as you.'

But, once again, the Zebra and the Eland just laughed at the old Crocodile. 'Come along, Zebra! It is time for us to go,' said the Eland.

The Zebra turned to the Crocodile and said: 'Goodbye, Crocodile, see you next time.' And with that, the Crocodile watched the Zebra and the Eland gallop off in a cloud of dust.

'Wait for me, I am coming with you!' the Crocodile called out. But they had disappeared, leaving only their footprints in the sand. The Crocodile looked at the ground and decided to follow their tracks.

The Crocodile began to walk, but he was very slow. It was not long before he started to feel hot and tired. This was the first time that the Crocodile had ever left the river, and he was really beginning to miss the cool water. When he could not go on any longer, the Crocodile decided to lie in the shade of a tree. The more time he spent under the tree, the more tired he felt.

'Eland and Zebra were right. I cannot go to the bush. I must return to the river,' he said to himself. After a little while the Crocodile tried to stand up, but he was too hot and tired to move. 'Oh, no, what am I going to do?' he moaned.

Just then, along came the Hare. 'Hey, old man, what are you doing so far away from the river?' asked the Hare.

When the Crocodile told the Hare what had happened, the Hare began to chuckle: 'What an old fool you are! But maybe I can help you.'

The Hare tried to lift the Crocodile, but he was very heavy. The Crocodile said: 'Please do not leave me here, Hare. I know I have been very stubborn and foolish.'

The Crocodile looked so hot and tired that the Hare felt sorry for him and decided to help him. 'Leave it to me, old man,' he said, as he set off to find someone to help him move the Crocodile back to the river.

The Hare was running as fast as he could when, without any warning, he tripped and fell to the ground. When he tried to stand up, he felt something pushing down hard on him. The Hare looked up and, to his dismay, he saw the Hyena grinning down at him.

'Well, well, what have we here?' said the Hyena, as he stood pressing his foot hard into the Hare's back. Once again the Hare tried to stand up, but the Hyena pressed his foot down harder and said: 'Tut! Tut! You are not going anywhere, little Hare. I have not eaten for days and you are going to be a tasty treat.'

The Hare began to tremble. He knew he had to think fast. 'Wait!' he cried out. 'You are very hungry, and I am only a small Hare. I can take you to where Crocodile is dying under a tree. Would you not like to eat him instead?' asked the Hare.

The Hyena stroked his chin and said: 'Mmm ... crocodile, you say. Yes, he is much bigger than you, but his skin is awfully hard and tough.'

Quickly the Hare replied: 'This is true, Hyena, but if you put him into the river to soak for a bit, his skin will become soft and tender enough to eat.'

The Hyena folded his arms and said: 'I like the sound of that, Hare. Take me to him, but this had better not be one of your tricks!'

The Hare shook his head and said: 'No; trust me, Hyena. If I am lying, then you can eat me instead.'

The Hyena smiled to himself. 'I will let Hare show me where the Crocodile is, and then I can eat them both,' he thought. Letting go of the Hare, the Hyena said: 'Well, come along then, I do not have all day.'

And, with that, the Hyena and the Hare made their way back to where the old Crocodile lay, too hot and tired to move.

When the Crocodile saw the Hare and the Hyena coming towards him, he began to worry. He knew how greedy the Hyena was. But as they stood in front of him, the Hare bent down close to the Crocodile and whispered in his ear: 'Do not be afraid. I have a plan to help you, but you must pretend that you are dying.'

The Crocodile had no idea what the Hare was up to, but he did as he was told. The Hyena was scared of the Crocodile's sharp teeth and wanted to make sure that he was really dying. The Hyena poked him with a stick, but the old Crocodile did not move.

The Hare began to laugh nervously and said: 'You see, Hyena. What did I tell you?'

The Hyena rubbed his hands together and grinned: 'Well done, Hare, but how am I going to carry him back to the river?'

The Hare smiled slyly and said: 'I will help you, and together we can carry him.'

And so, with the help of the Hare, the Hyena lifted up the old Crocodile and they began to walk. The Crocodile was very heavy and, after walking for a little bit, the Hyena became tired. When the Hare saw that the Hyena was becoming tired, he winked at the Crocodile and said to the Hyena: 'We should put Crocodile down and rest for a while.'

By now the Hyena was panting. 'I think we should, Hare,' he said, out of breath. When the Hyena felt he had rested long enough, they were on their way again.

Every so often the Hare would turn to the Hyena and say: 'Why do we not put the Crocodile down and rest for a bit?' With each step he took, the Crocodile felt heavier and heavier to the Hyena, so he never argued. Each time the Hare told him to rest, the Hyena would let go of the Crocodile and catch his breath.

As the sun was beginning to set, they saw that they were very close to the river. The Hare cried out: 'Look! We are almost there!' The Crocodile was so happy to see the river that he almost jumped for joy. But then he remembered what the Hare had told him, and stayed very still.

The Hyena was also pleased to see the river, and said: 'Finally! I am so hungry.' The Crocodile was scared when he heard these words, but he tried hard not to shake.

When they approached the river, the Hare said to the Hyena: 'We have been carrying the heavy Crocodile all day. Let's put him down and rest for a while.'

The Hyena thought to himself: 'Now is my chance. I do not need Hare any longer, now that we are close to the river. I will first eat Hare and I will eat Crocodile later.'

The Hyena gave the Hare a big smile and said: 'Thank you, Hare. You have been a great help, but I will no longer be needing your services.'

The Hare did not like the way that the Hyena was smiling at him. 'What is he up to?' thought the Hare to himself. But then, suddenly, the Hyena grabbed the Hare by his ears and was licking his lips.

'But I thought we had a deal!' the Hare cried out. 'You said you would not eat me if I showed you where Crocodile was.'

The Hyena laughed when he heard these words and said: 'You should know better than to believe anything I say, little Hare.'

Just as the Hyena was about to eat the Hare, the Crocodile, who had been lying very still, jumped up. The Hyena got such a fright when he saw that the Crocodile was actually alive that he dropped the Hare. And then the Crocodile opened up his huge mouth and, with one gulp, he swallowed the Hyena.

The Hare was so surprised by what had happened that he could not speak. When he stopped shaking he turned to the Crocodile and said: 'Thank you, old man. You saved my life.'

The Crocodile smiled shyly and said: 'You saved my life too, Hare.'

The Hare grinned and said: 'Well, I guess that makes us friends!'

The Crocodile's eyes lit up when he heard this. 'Do you really mean that?' he asked the Hare.

The Hare slapped him on the back and said: 'But of course I do, you old fool!'

The Crocodile turned to the Hare and asked: 'Will you come and visit me, then?'

The Hare replied: 'Do not worry, Crocodile. I promise I will come and visit you so that you never have to leave the river again.'

The Crocodile could have cried for joy as he climbed into the river and felt the cool water on his hot, dry skin. The Hare kept his promise and went to see the Crocodile every day. The old Crocodile stayed near the river from then on, and he never felt lonely again.

WHY THE ZEBRA HAS STRIPES

Based on the collection Bushman Stories, E.W. Thomas (1950). Oxford University Press:
Cape Town, London and New York.

During the time of the First People, the Gemsbok and the Zebra looked very different to the way they look today. For a start, the Zebra did not have any stripes, but she did have long, beautiful horns. This is the story of how the Zebra lost her horns and got her stripes.

Each day at sunset, all the animals would meet at the waterhole to drink. The Zebra used to spend hours looking at herself in the water. She was very proud of her long horns, and never tired of looking at them. But what the Zebra loved most was hearing the comments of all the other animals about how beautiful her horns were.

The Gemsbok used to watch the Zebra while she was drinking, and think to herself: 'Zebra is so lucky to have horns. I wish I could have them, even if it was just for one day.' For, you see, the Gemsbok did not have horns, and she was very jealous of the Zebra. When she went to the waterhole to drink, the Gemsbok would look at herself in the water and sigh. 'Oh, look at me. I must be the most dull and boring of all the animals,' she would say to her reflection. One day, the Gemsbok decided she was going to ask the Zebra if she could wear her horns for a day.

She waited and waited at the waterhole for the Zebra to come. At sunset, when the Zebra bent down to drink some water, the Gemsbok said to the Zebra: 'Look how much more beautiful you are than me. I would also like to have horns like you.' The Gemsbok knew that the Zebra liked to be admired.

'Yes, they are rather grand, are they not?' the Zebra said, looking at her reflection.

Then the Gemsbok looked at Zebra with big, sad eyes and asked: 'Please will you let me wear your horns for a day?'

The Zebra threw her head back and laughed: 'Oh, no, my good friend. I cannot possibly go without my horns, even for one day.' The Zebra did not want to look as dull and boring as the Gemsbok, but when she saw how sad the Gemsbok looked, she felt sorry for her. The Zebra was quiet for a while, and then turned to the Gemsbok and said: 'I have given it some thought, and I will let you wear one of my horns.'

The Gemsbok replied: 'Zebra, you are so vain and proud! You will not let me wear your horns, even for one day!'

This made the Zebra angry. 'You are very ungrateful!' she scolded the Gemsbok, 'and, for that, I won't even give you one horn,' she added before galloping off.

The Gemsbok lay down next to the waterhole and began to cry. She had lost her chance of ever wearing the Zebra's horns. After a little while, the Gemsbok stopped crying and thought to herself: 'If the Zebra will not lend me her horns, I will have to just have to steal them.'

And, with that, the Gemsbok jumped up and went off to find the Zebra. When she found the Zebra, she was at the river, looking at herself in the water. The Gemsbok hid behind a tree and waited for the Zebra to go to sleep. When the Gemsbok was sure that the Zebra was fast asleep, she quietly crept up to her. When she was close enough, she took a deep breath and then snatched the horns off the Zebra's head! The Zebra woke up with a start, but the Gemsbok was too fast. Before the Zebra could catch her, the Gemsbok had disappeared into the night.

When she could not see the Gemsbok any longer, the Zebra felt her head where her horns had been. 'My beautiful long horns! They are gone!' she cried out in despair, but there was nothing to be done.

The next day, the Zebra woke up and went to look at herself in the river. When she saw how dull and boring she looked, she said: 'No one will admire me now. I wish I had not been too proud to let Gemsbok wear my horns for one day.'

She let out a big sigh, because the Zebra knew that the Gemsbok was much faster than her, and that she would never be able steal her horns back. 'Maybe, after a little while, the Gemsbok will grow tired of my horns and give them back to me,' she said to herself.

After she thought about it for a little longer, the proud Zebra decided that she did not want to see the other animals until the Gemsbok gave back her horns. And so it was on that day that the Zebra set off to find another waterhole from which to drink. After walking all day in the hot sun, the Zebra began to grow thirsty. Just when the sun was about to set and she thought she would never find anywhere to drink, the Zebra saw a waterhole. 'Thank goodness!' she exclaimed. When she reached the waterhole, the Zebra saw that there were no other animals around. For the first time since she had lost her horns, the Zebra was pleased: 'At last I have found a place to drink where no one else will see how dull and boring I look without my horns,' she thought to herself as she lowered her head to drink.

But before she could even take one sip of water, the Zebra heard a voice behind her cry out: 'Who dares to drink at my waterhole?' The

Zebra was so frightened that she jumped up into the air and fell down with a crash! When she looked up, the Baboon was standing over her. 'I am the master of this waterhole,' he shouted as he pounded hard on his chest.

The Zebra was so surprised to see anyone, especially someone so angry, that she did not know what else to do but run off. When the Zebra was sure that the Baboon was not following her, she stopped to catch her breath.

As if from nowhere, the Zebra heard a voice say: 'I would not try that again if I was you.' The Zebra quickly turned around and there stood the Ostrich. Next to her was her sister, the Crane.

'Phew!' she said, wiping her forehead. 'I thought you were Baboon.'

The Crane leaned forward and said to the Zebra: 'I say, you look odd. Where are your horns?'

The Ostrich looked over her sister's shoulder and added: 'You do look awfully dull without them, if you do not mind me saying so.'

Feeling herself grow red with shame as they both began to giggle, the Zebra covered her head and said: 'You nasty sisters! Leave me alone. Gemsbok has them, and I am waiting for her to give them back.'

The Ostrich fluttered her eyelashes and said: 'Come now, there's no need to be so cross. We are just trying to help you.'

The Zebra kicked up some sand and replied: 'I do not need your help. I am going to wait for Baboon to leave the waterhole. When he does, I will be able to drink the water.'

The Crane and the Ostrich looked at each other and rolled their eyes. 'You had better listen to us and go back to your own waterhole,' warned the Ostrich.

'Baboon has put a curse on the waterhole. It will poison anyone who tries to drink from it,' added the Crane.

The Zebra laughed and said: 'How silly you both are! You do not really believe that, do you?'

The Ostrich and the Crane both nodded their heads. 'It is true! Why do you think there were no other animals drinking at the waterhole?' said the Crane.

But the Zebra did not want to listen to the sisters and, without even saying goodbye, she galloped off. 'How rude!' said the Ostrich.

'How rude, indeed!' replied her sister.

The next day, the Zebra returned to the waterhole. Hiding behind some bushes, she watched the Baboon. All day she waited, but he never left the waterhole. The Zebra watched as the Baboon lay around in the warm sun, hardly moving, except to drink or to scratch himself. At night, the Baboon would warm himself at the fire, but still he did not leave the waterhole. And, just as the Ostrich and the Crane had said, the Zebra did not see even one animal try to drink at the waterhole.

But the Zebra did not want to give up so easily. 'I do not believe that the water is poisoned,' thought the Zebra. 'If Baboon can drink from it, then so can I.' The next day she went back and watched the Baboon. Once again the lazy Baboon slept in the sun, but he still did not leave the waterhole. On the third day, the Zebra was in luck. The Baboon moved away from the rock he was lying on to look for berries and roots to eat.

'Now is my chance,' whispered the Zebra quietly to herself. When she could not see the Baboon any longer, the Zebra left her hiding place and went to drink from the waterhole.

The Ostrich and the Crane walked by and saw the Zebra drinking. 'Stop! Stop!' they yelled.

'You will die,' cried out the Crane.

But to their surprise, the Zebra drank from the water and did not die. In fact, she looked very happy indeed. Just then, the Zebra heard the Ostrich shout: 'Look out, Baboon is behind you!'

But the Zebra laughed and said: 'You will not fool me again, you silly bird,' and carried on drinking. The Ostrich covered her eyes as she saw the Baboon tackle the Zebra.

'How dare you drink from my waterhole!' he barked, as the Zebra went tumbling down to the ground. The Zebra tried to stand up and run away, but the Baboon was too strong. Before she could stand up, the Baboon picked her up and threw the Zebra hard onto the ground. The Ostrich and the Crane let out a gasp as they saw that the Zebra had landed right in the Baboon's fire. The Ostrich and the Crane could not stand to watch any longer, so they rushed towards the Baboon, flapping their wings and hissing.

'Leave Zebra alone, you brute, or we will scratch your eyes out!' cried the Ostrich.

The Baboon knew that he was no match for their long legs and sharp claws, so he ran off, screaming: 'You crazy sisters! Leave me alone!'

The Crane and the Ostrich giggled to each other when they saw how scared the Baboon looked.

'Oh, my back hurts,' moaned the Zebra as she staggered up from the fiery ground.

'Look how beautiful she looks!' exclaimed the Crane. The Zebra looked around to see who the Crane was talking about, but she did not see anyone else. When the Crane saw the Zebra looking around, she said: 'I am talking about you, Zebra. Look at your back.' The Zebra looked, and could not believe her eyes. The fire that the Baboon had pushed her into had burnt her and left black stripes all over her back! The Zebra went to have a better look at her reflection in the water.

'Hooray! I am not dull and boring any more. I do not care if the Gemsbok keeps my horns, now that I have these beautiful stripes,' she said and galloped off to show the rest of the animals. As for the Baboon, he never came back to that waterhole and, from then on, thanks to the Zebra, all the animals that passed by could drink from it.

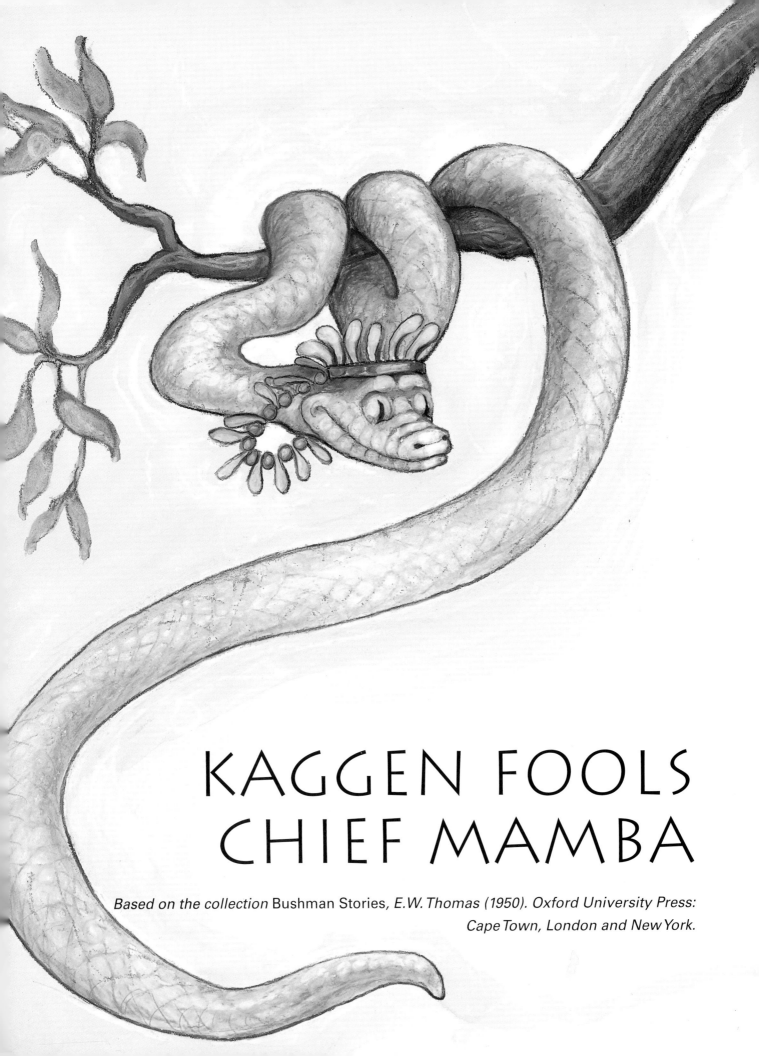

KAGGEN FOOLS CHIEF MAMBA

Based on the collection Bushman Stories, *E.W. Thomas (1950). Oxford University Press:* Cape Town, London and New York.

One day, Kaggen's Walking Stick was very bored. He had not been on an adventure for a long time and was fed up with having nothing to do. The Walking Stick paced up and down: 'Tap! Tap!'

After a few hours, the Bag said to the Walking Stick: 'Oh my friend, must you make such a racket?' The Bag could not understand why the Walking Stick was not happy just to lie in the warm sun.

The Walking Stick stopped and explained: 'I am not like you, old Bag. I am tired of sitting around all day, doing nothing. When will Kaggen take us somewhere again?'

Just then, Kaggen arrived and called out: 'Get ready, everybody!'

'Yippee! We are going on a journey,' added the Shoes, who were already on Kaggen's feet.

The Walking Stick could not believe his luck. 'Finally!' he said to Kaggen, and then asked: 'Where are we going?'

Kaggen was just about to answer the Walking Stick, when the Shoes shouted out: 'To see Mamba, chief of all the snakes in the land!'

When the Bag heard this, he let out a deep groan and said: 'Oh no! Oh dear me, not Chief Mamba. He lives so far away, on the other side of the hills.'

The Walking Stick poked the Bag and laughed happily: 'That's right, old Bag, no more dozing in the sun for you.' And, with that, Kaggen hitched the Bag onto his back, grabbed the Walking Stick and set out to visit Chief Mamba.

As Kaggen and his belongings approached the hills, they could hear them grumbling and groaning to one another. For you see, at that time, all the hills in the land were joined together. There was no way to pass through the hills, so if anyone ever needed to travel to the other side of the hills, they always had to climb over them. And because the hills were joined together, they argued all day long.

'I am tired of hearing you complain all the time,' one hill would say to the other.

'Well, if you don't like it, why don't you move on?' the other hill would reply crossly.

'Why should I move? Why don't you?' And so it would go on.

That day, Kaggen and his belongings stopped to rest at the bottom of one of the hills. They had been walking for most of the day, and were very tired.

'I wish we did not have to climb over the hills,' complained the Shoes, huffing and puffing.

'If only there was some way we could pass through,' thought Kaggen to himself, and decided to take a closer look. Just then, Kaggen noticed a small gap between two of the hills. Feeling rather pleased with himself, the little mantis tried to squeeze through. But, even as he tried, the strangest thing happened. The hills quickly moved closer together and closed the gap.

'Ouch! You almost squashed me,' Kaggen said to the hills, and rubbed his head. 'But I am not giving up so easily,' he yelled at them. Once again, Kaggen tried to squeeze through the small gap between the hills. But once again, the hills quickly moved together so that Kaggen could not pass through. Kaggen tried over and over again until he was completely out of breath and fell to the ground.

'You hills are such a nuisance!' said Kaggen, gasping for breath. He shook his fist in the air: 'You are making our journey very difficult, because you will not let us pass through. All day we have to listen to you moaning at one another. What is the point of being close together if you just fight all the time?'

After Kaggen had stopped shouting at them, the hills became very quiet. After a little while, one of the hills said in a deep, rumbling voice: 'Perhaps Kaggen is right; we would probably all argue much less if we were not joined to each other.' There was a murmering of agreement among the rest of the hills.

'But who is going to move?' asked one of the long, tall hills.

'I think you should move,' replied the short, rocky hill.

'Why don't you move?' added another.

Eventually, all the hills were shouting at once. Kaggen held his hands over his ears and cried out: 'Will all of you please keep quiet!' While the hills were arguing, Kaggen had thought of a plan. 'If you cannot decide among yourselves who will move, then I think it is only fair that you all move.' He pointed at one group of hills and said: 'You move to the left.' Pointing at the rest of the hills, Kaggen said: 'As for all of you, I want you to move to the right.'

And with those words, much to Kaggen's surprise, the hills began to move slowly away from one another. Some of the hills moved only a little, while the rest moved very far away from the others. Kaggen and his belongings did not want to waste any more time, and were soon on their way again. From then on, thanks to Kaggen, the hills always allowed everyone to pass through them, and were never heard moaning again.

Now that they did not have to climb over all the hills, it did not take Kaggen and his friends much longer to reach the house of Chief Mamba. At that time, the Mamba was chief of all the snakes in the land. Many animals feared him, because he was so rich and powerful.

As they neared Chief Mamba's house, Kaggen whispered: 'Do you have the feeling that we are being watched?'

'That's because we are!' whispered the Walking Stick.

'Look in the grass!' exclaimed the Shoes, trembling.

And, sure enough, there were hundreds of eyes peering out at them. One of the pairs of eyes appeared to be hissing. The Shoes, the Walking Stick and the Bag all hid behind Kaggen.

'W-we are n-not s-scared,' stammered Kaggen, who was trying very hard to be brave. The hissing grew louder, and was now all around them. Kaggen cleared his throat and said in his bravest voice: 'We are here to see the Mamba, chief of all the snakes in the land.' Just then, the longest snake they had ever seen slithered out of a deep hole and hissed: 'Ssss! Ssso little mantissss, what do you want from the chief of all the sssnakes in the land?'

Kaggen replied: 'Chief Mamba, you are very rich. You have many cows and farms. I have come to ask you for a few cows so that I, too, can have milk when I am hungry.'

Chief Mamba slithered closer to Kaggen and began to wrap himself around Kaggen's legs. 'Ssso, little mantisss. If I give you my cowsss, what are you going to give me in return?'

Kaggen scratched his head and thought hard. 'I do not have anything to give you in return, Chief Mamba, but I am sure there is something I can do for you.'

Chief Mamba carried on slithering around Kaggen's legs: 'Actually, little mantisss, there isss sssomething you can do for me. If you help me build a kraal for my cowsss, I will give you two cowsss.'

Kaggen was delighted and said: 'Leave it to me, Chief Mamba!'

As soon as Chief Mamba had disappeared back into his hole, the Walking Stick turned to Kaggen: 'You never said anything about doing any work, Kaggen! You tricked us into coming here.'

Kaggen replied: 'I am sorry, friends, but you would have never come with me if I had told you we would have to work for Chief Mamba. It is only one little job, and then we will be off home with two cows of our very own.'

The Walking Stick let out a big sigh: 'Oh, very well, Kaggen. I suppose you are right.'

Kaggen and his friends worked hard all day making the kraal. Finally, late in the afternoon, Chief Mamba came slithering out of his deep hole. 'Ssso little mantisss, you have done a good job. You must be hungry and tired. Why do you not sssleep here tonight and tomorrow you can return home?'

Kaggen looked at the sun as it was setting and said: 'It will be dark soon, maybe it would be a good idea to sleep here tonight and leave early in the morning.'

Wrapping himself around Kaggen's legs, Chief Mamba said: 'If you are going to stay here with me tonight, would you be so kind as to make me some food, Kaggen?'

Kaggen was tired after working all day and did not feel like cooking food for Chief Mamba, but he really wanted the cows, so he answered: 'It will be a pleasure.' And, once again, the Mamba slithered back down into his hole.

When Kaggen had finished cooking, he shouted down the hole: 'Chief Mamba, your dinner is ready.'

Chief Mamba slithered out and wrapped himself even tighter around Kaggen's legs. 'Please will you feed me,' he asked Kaggen.

By this time, Kaggen began to feel a little cross with Chief Mamba, but then he thought about the two cows and said: 'Yes Chief Mamba, I will feed you.'

Once Chief Mamba had finished eating, he said to Kaggen: 'You must be cold; will you please gather some wood to make a fire?'

As Kaggen went off to collect wood, he said to his belongings: 'Do you think Chief Mamba is ever going to give me two of his cows?'

The Walking Stick was very angry with Kaggen: 'You involved us in this mess, Kaggen, and you are going to have to help us out of it.'

Kaggen was quiet. He was trying to find a way to escape from Chief Mamba and keep his cows. Just then the Bag said in his slow, deep voice: 'Chief Mamba is very clever, but he is also very proud.'

These words gave Kaggen an idea. When Kaggen returned with the firewood, Chief Mamba said to him: 'Please will you light a fire?'

Kaggen forced himself to smile and said: 'Of course, Chief Mamba.'

Once he had the fire going, Kaggen said to Chief Mamba: 'You are very rich and powerful but can you jump over this fire?'

Chief Mamba hissed back at Kaggen: 'Of course I can. I am Mamba, chief of all the sssnakes in the land.'

And before Chief Mamba could say anything else, Kaggen jumped over the fire and said: 'Very well, Chief Mamba, then show me that you can jump over the fire, just as I have done.'

The Bag was right; Chief Mamba was very proud and did not want the rest of the snakes to see that he could not jump over the fire. And so Chief Mamba tried as hard as he could, but instead of jumping over the fire, he fell right into it! Kaggen laughed when he saw Chief Mamba trying to roll himself out of the fire. 'You may be rich and powerful, but you must also be stupid to try to jump when you know that you cannot,' he said to Chief Mamba.

And then, before Chief Mamba had a chance to call the other snakes, Kaggen quickly jumped up, grabbed two cows from the kraal and vanished into the darkness.

WHY THE OSTRICH HAS NO HORNS

A story based on the version that appears in Living Legends of a Dying Culture, *Coral Fourie (1994). Ekogilde: Hartbeespoort.*

In San mythology there are different stories that explain why the world is as it is or why animals look a certain way. This is because most of the stories are preserved and passed on orally, so they sometimes change over time as they are told and re-told. This is another version of the story of how the Ostrich lost her horns.

There was a time, long ago, when the Ostrich was one of the most beautiful animals in the land. Her feathers were the colours of the rainbow, and she had long eyelashes that fluttered when as talked. But most beautiful of all was the pair of horns that stood proudly on her head. The Ostrich would spend all day strutting up and down, showing off her coloured feathers and long horns. Whenever any of the other animals passed, she would spread her colourful wings and toss her head from side to side. The animals would gasp and go: 'Ooh!' and 'Ah!' when they saw the Ostrich. 'Ostrich is so beautiful,' one would comment to the other.

The Ostrich would then flutter her eyelashes and pretend to hide behind her wing. 'Do you really think I am beautiful?' she always asked. The Ostrich knew that she was beautiful, indeed, but she never tired of people telling her so. Of all the animals, the Gemsbok was the only one who never told the Ostrich she was beautiful. He was a pale and boring-looking animal and was jealous of the Ostrich. The Gemsbok wanted the Ostrich's beautiful horns for himself.

'The Ostrich is so vain. It is not fair that she has both beautiful feathers and long horns,' he thought, as he watched the Ostrich from a distance. One day, the Gemsbok was fed up with wishing that he had the Ostrich's horns. He decided to do something about it and trick the Ostrich into giving him her long, beautiful horns.

The Gemsbok strolled over to the Ostrich and, in a loud voice for all to hear, he challenged her: 'You may be beautiful, Ostrich, but can you run fast, really fast?'

The Ostrich laughed in a high voice and answered: 'Hee! Hee! You silly Gemsbok, look at how long my legs are. Of course I can run fast!'

The Gemsbok looked up and down at the Ostrich's legs and said: 'Yes, they are very long, but that does not mean that you can run fast.' The Ostrich did not know what to say next. She was used to others admiring her beautiful colours and her long horns. This was the first time anyone

had ever asked her if she could run fast. The Ostrich was quiet for a moment, and then she said: 'I know! I will run, so that you can see how fast I am.'

The Gemsbok shook his head: 'No, I think we should have a race to see who is the fastest.'

The Ostrich thought to herself: 'I am sure that I will win the race. Then I will be the most beautiful and the fastest of all the animals in the land.' She turned to the Gemsbok: 'Very well, Gemsbok. I will race you.'

When the rest of the animals heard that the Gemsbok and the Ostrich were going to have a race, they were very excited. It was not long before a large crowd had come to watch the race.

The Ostrich and the Gemsbok stretched their legs as they prepared for the race. By then, so many animals had gathered to watch them race that there was a lot of pushing and shoving going on among them to reach the front. 'Watch where you are going, Elephant, you almost crushed me!' cried out the Hare.

The Elephant looked down and saw the Hare underneath him. 'Sorry, Hare. I cannot see a thing with all of them sitting up there,' he said, pointing to his head. The Hare looked up at the Elephant and there he saw the Bush-Bird, the Mouse and the Bees all squashed together on top of the Elephant's head.

Every now and then, the Ostrich would lift one of her colourful wings and wave to the crowd. As the Gemsbok watched the Ostrich, he smiled to himself and said: 'Soon I will be more beautiful than the Ostrich, and *I* will be the one that all the animals admire.' He turned to the Ostrich: 'Are you ready?'

But the Ostrich was so busy blowing kisses to the crowd that she did not even hear the Gemsbok. 'Thank you all for coming,' the Ostrich called out to the animals in a proud voice.

The Gemsbok cleared his throat and said: 'Ahem … Ostrich … are you ready to start the race?'

The Ostrich turned around and fluttered her eyelashes at the Gemsbok: 'Do not be so impatient, my friend; I am almost ready.'

Then the Ostrich stretched her neck so that her horns looked even longer. 'Ooh!' and 'Ah!,' went the animals.

The Gemsbok tapped his foot loudly. The Ostrich rolled her eyes and said: 'All right, all right. I am ready now.'

'Wait! Wait!' yelled out a voice from the crowd. The Gemsbok and the Ostrich both turned around to see who it was. They saw that it was the Giraffe, running towards them.

'This had better be important, Giraffe. Can you not see that we are about to start the race?' said the Gemsbok, and stamped his foot hard on the ground.

'I know, Gemsbok, but if this is to be a proper and fair race, you need someone to judge the race.'

'The Giraffe is right,' the Monkey called out from the crowd. Everyone began nodding their heads in agreement.

The Gemsbok sighed and said: 'Very well, but for goodness sake, let's continue with the race.'

The Giraffe drew a line in the sand and said: 'Both of you stand behind this line. Whoever touches that thorn tree first, wins the race.'

When the Ostrich and the Gemsbok were both at the starting line, the Giraffe called out: 'Ready, steady, and go!' The crowd cheered the Ostrich on when they saw how fast she could run but, after a little while, they all saw that she was no match for the Gemsbok. No matter how fast she ran, she could not catch up with the Gemsbok. 'The Gemsbok has won the race!' yelled out the Giraffe, as the Gemsbok touched the thorn tree. 'Three cheers for Gemsbok,' added the Giraffe.

'Hip! Hip! Hooray!' the animals cried out together.

When the Ostrich heard all the animals clapping and cheering for the Gemsbok she began to cry. She was very disappointed. 'This is so unfair!' she cried out. 'I am the one for whom you should be cheering and clapping.'

Everyone went very quiet when they heard these words. The Ostrich could see that all the animals felt sad for her. 'I do not want them to feel sorry for me,' she thought to herself, 'I want them to admire me.'

And then, to everyone's great surprise, the Gemsbok said to the Ostrich: 'You are right, the race was not fair.'

The Giraffe was puzzled: 'I am the judge and I saw with my very own eyes that you won the race, fair and square.'

The Gemsbok shook his head: 'No, I think we should race again.' He turned to the Ostrich and said: 'Your horns are too heavy for your thin neck and two skinny legs. I have four strong legs, so it is only fair that I wear your horns for the race.'

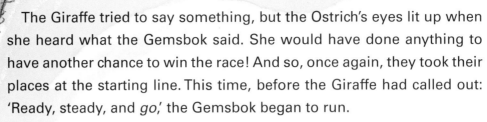

The Giraffe tried to say something, but the Ostrich's eyes lit up when she heard what the Gemsbok said. She would have done anything to have another chance to win the race! And so, once again, they took their places at the starting line. This time, before the Giraffe had called out: 'Ready, steady, and *go*,' the Gemsbok began to run.

The crowd gasped in horror as they saw that the Gemsbok was not even heading towards the finish line. He was running away with the Ostrich's horns. 'My horns!' shrieked the Ostrich as she ran after him.

The Gemsbok looked over his shoulder and laughed: 'Come and get them, Ostrich!' After a little while, the Ostrich felt the ground becoming harder and harder under her feet. The Ostrich had much softer feet than the Gemsbok, and could not run on stones they way he could. The Gemsbok knew this, and had planned it all along.

The Ostrich yelled out: 'Stop! Stop!' But the Gemsbok kept running. Finally, the stones began to hurt Ostrich's feet too much, and she had to stop. When the Gemsbok saw that the Ostrich had stopped running, he also stopped. They were both very out of breath. While she huffed and puffed, the Ostrich bent down and picked up a stone. She threw it at the Gemsbok and shouted: 'Give me back my horns!'

'Ouch!' exclaimed the Gemsbok as the stone hit him on the head. The Ostrich picked up another stone and threw it at the Gemsbok. But this time he was ready, and ducked when he saw it flying towards him.

'Sorry, Ostrich. I am not giving them back.' This made the Ostrich furious. She bent down to look for a bigger stone to throw at the Gemsbok. But when she looked up again, he had vanished!

The Ostrich fell to the floor and began to cry all over her beautiful feathers. 'What am I going to do without my horns?' she sobbed. 'No one will think I am beautiful again.' The Ostrich cried for hours and hours. When she grew tired of crying, she thought to herself: 'Maybe the Gemsbok was right and my horns are too long and heavy for my thin neck and two skinny legs.'

Just then, the Bush-Bird came flying by. 'Do not be so sad, Ostrich. You do not need your horns to be beautiful,' said the Bush-Bird.

The Ostrich wiped her eyes: 'Do you really think so?' she asked, hiding behind her wing. The Bush-Bird nodded. The Ostrich smiled and said: 'I think you are right, little one. Please go and find the Gemsbok and tell him I am not angry any more. I want us to be friends.'

The Bush-Bird flapped her wings: 'You can count on me, Ostrich,' she said as she flew off. When the Bush-Bird found the Gemsbok, he was resting under the shade of a tree. He had been running for a long time to escape from the Ostrich, and was very tired. The Bush-Bird called out: 'Hello, Gemsbok, I have a message for you from Ostrich.'

The Gemsbok looked up when he heard the Bush-Bird and answered: 'Whatever it is, I am not giving back her horns.'

The Bush-Bird flew down and sat in the tree: 'Do not worry, Gemsbok, that is not why I am here.'

The Gemsbok was surprised when he heard that the Ostrich wanted to be friends with him, even though he had stolen her horns. This made the Gemsbok feel bad about what he had done.

'The Ostrich is so kind to let me keep her horns. I wish I could do something for her in return,' he said to the Bush-Bird. Just then, the Gemsbok had an idea. 'I know! Now that I have these long horns, I can protect Ostrich,' he said out loud. He turned to the Bush-Bird and said: 'Go and tell Ostrich that we will be friends and I will always be near to make sure that she is never harmed.'

The Bush-Bird did what the Gemsbok asked and from that day on, the Ostrich and the Gemsbok were, to everyone's great surprise, the very best of friends.

KAGGEN AND THE MAGIC BIRD

A story based on the version that appears in The Mantis and his Friends: Bushman Folklore, *D.F. Bleek (1923). Maskew Miller: Cape Town.*

Kaggen held up his new bow and arrow and said: 'There! It is finished.'

The Walking Stick tapped the Bag lying next to him and whispered: 'Kaggen has been busy the whole day making a new bow and arrow. You know what this means, don't you?'

The Bag first groaned softly and then answered: 'Yes, I do. Kaggen is going to want to steal eggs from Ostrich again.'

The Shoes let out a giggle. 'And what is so funny?' asked the Walking Stick, annoyed.

'Hee! Hee! Remember how cross Ostrich was the last time Kaggen stole eggs from her?' said the Shoes softly, so that Kaggen would not hear. The Ostrich had been very angry indeed. Kaggen had to grow feathers and fly away to escape her long, sharp claws. It made the Bag tremble with fear, just thinking about how the Ostrich had chased them as she hissed and waved her wings wildly.

'I do not think it is funny at all,' the Bag said to the Shoes.

'Next time we might not be so lucky,' added the Walking Stick.

Just then Kaggen called out: 'Come on everybody, it is time to try out my new bow and arrow!' Only the Shoes jumped up. The Bag and the Walking Stick lay very still. Kaggen nudged the Walking Stick and the Bag with his toe: 'Did you not hear me?'

The Walking Stick answered: 'We heard you, Kaggen, and we do not think you should be shooting your arrow at Ostrich or stealing her eggs.'

Kaggen threw back his head and laughed: 'Look how scared you both are!' Then he bent down to pick up the Bag and the Walking Stick and said: 'Do not worry, my friends. I am too fast for Ostrich. She will never catch me.'

But the Walking Stick and the Bag quickly moved away. Kaggen stamped his foot and said: 'Fine, stay here! Just remember, I will not be sharing any of those delicious eggs with either of you.' And with that, Kaggen stormed off, leaving the Bag and the Walking Stick behind.

'You will be sorry, Kaggen!' the Walking Stick called out after him. Kaggen turned around and pretended to shoot an arrow at the Walking Stick. The Walking Stick yelled as he jumped out the way, which made Kaggen laugh.

The Bag said to the Walking Stick: 'Do not be angry, my friend. Kaggen will soon learn his lesson.' They watched Kaggen until he disappeared into the distance.

Kaggen was cross that the Walking Stick and the Bag did not want to come with him. 'Those cowards – I do not need them anyway!' he exclaimed, as he kicked the ground and covered the Shoes with sand. The Shoes began to cough. Kaggen looked down and said: 'Oops, sorry little friends,' and bent down to dust them off. Then he gave the Shoes a pat, and added: 'Soon we will be eating delicious Ostrich eggs.'

After a short while, Kaggen saw that they were close to where the Ostrich had made her nest. 'We must not let Ostrich hear us,' he whispered to the Shoes. The Shoes began to feel afraid when they saw the Ostrich. They had forgotten how big and tall she was. Kaggen crouched behind a tree and aimed his bow and arrow at the Ostrich, who was sitting on her nest. The Ostrich shrieked as the arrow flew past her and just missed her head. She jumped up off her nest as Kaggen shot another arrow at her. When Kaggen saw that the Ostrich had left her nest, he quickly ran and grabbed two of her eggs.

'You naughty mantis! Leave my eggs alone!' screamed the Ostrich. Then she began to hiss loudly and moved threateningly towards Kaggen with her long claws.

'Hurry Kaggen!' yelled the Shoes.

'Hold on tight!' cried Kaggen, as he flew up into the air and left the Ostrich behind, hissing and flapping her wings.

When Kaggen was sure that he was out of the Ostrich's reach, he flew down to the ground to rest. 'Phew! That was close – Ostrich almost caught us,' said Kaggen, and wiped his head.

The Shoes were still trembling: 'Her c-c-claws are s-s-so l-l-long,' they stammered.

Kaggen broke the shell of one egg and said: 'Do not worry, we are safe now.' And, with that, Kaggen and the Shoes began to eat. When they had finished, Kaggen said: 'Mmm ... that was delicious,' and rubbed his stomach. 'I wish I had taken more than two eggs,' thought Kaggen, for he was a greedy mantis.

'Can we go home now?' asked the Shoes. They were very tired after the adventure.

Kaggen answered: 'Yes. I am also tired. We can eat this other egg once we are home.' And so Kaggen and the Shoes began to make their way home. Suddenly, Kaggen saw something that made him stop short. Just ahead of them was the most beautiful bird he had ever seen.

Her whole body was covered in shimmering silver feathers that made a soft tinkling sound whenever she moved.

'It is the Magic Bird,' gasped the Shoes.

'It is said that she lays silver eggs,' they told Kaggen.

When Kaggen heard this, he moved closer to take a better look. 'I would like to have a silver egg,' thought Kaggen to himself. And so he crouched down and aimed his bow and arrow at the Magic Bird. To Kaggen's amazement, as soon as the arrow touched one of the silver feathers, the arrow turned around and flew back at him.

'We should leave the Magic Bird alone,' said the Shoes softly. But by then Kaggen was even more determined to take one of her eggs. He was just about to shoot another arrow when the Magic Bird suddenly opened her wings and, with a soft tinkling sound, flew away.

'Look, there are her silver eggs!' cried Kaggen. He could not believe his luck! The Magic Bird had left her nest, and now he could take as many silver eggs as he wanted.

Kaggen crept up to the nest and was just about to grab an egg, when the Shoes cried out: 'Don't, Kaggen! If those eggs belong to the Magic Bird, they must have special powers. You do not know what will happen if you steal them.'

But Kaggen would not listen to their warning. As he stretched out his hand to touch the silver eggs, Kaggen said to the Shoes: 'Do not worry so much. The Magic Bird is gone, so nothing will happen to me.'

No sooner had he said that than Kaggen saw that one of the silver eggs was stuck to his hand. No matter how hard he tried, Kaggen could not remove the egg from his hand! The poor little mantis tried everything. First, he shook his hand as hard as he could. Then he jumped up and down, waving his arms in the air, but still the egg stayed stuck to his hand.

The Shoes tried hard not to laugh, but Kaggen looked very funny jumping around with an egg stuck to his hand!

'Stop laughing!' shouted Kaggen, but the Shoes could not help themselves. After a little while Kaggen grew tired and gave up. 'Come on, Shoes, let's go home. Maybe the Bag or the Walking Stick can help me,' he said.

When Kaggen was close to home, the Bag saw him and called out to the Walking Stick: 'I see Kaggen, and it looks as if he is carrying a silver egg.' The Walking Stick jumped up and watched as Kaggen approached.

The Walking Stick began to laugh: 'I do not think that Kaggen is *carrying* a silver egg. It looks more as though he is stuck to it!'

The Bag saw that the Walking Stick was, indeed, right. When Kaggen was close enough, the Walking Stick tapped the egg and said: 'Well, well. Look who seems to have found himself in a spot of trouble with the Magic Bird.'

Kaggen opened his eyes wide and asked the Walking Stick: 'What do you know about the Magic Bird?'

The Walking Stick first winked at the Bag and then he said to Kaggen: 'I have heard that if you ever touch an egg belonging to the Magic Bird, it will become stuck to you forever.'

Kaggen's mouth dropped open: 'Forever! It cannot be true, there must be a way to remove this egg!'

In a sad voice the Walking Stick replied: 'I am sorry, Kaggen, but there really is no way to break the magic spell.' Kaggen sat down on the ground and began to cry. 'This would never have happened if I was not so greedy. I should not have stolen the egg in the first place,' Kaggen said, in between sobs.

'Does this mean you have learnt your lesson, Kaggen?' asked the Bag in a slow, deep voice.

Kaggen nodded and replied: 'Yes, I have, but now it is too late.'

The Walking Stick tapped Kaggen on the shoulder and shook his head: 'Perhaps it is not too late, my friend.'

Kaggen wiped his eyes and said: 'What do you mean?'

The Walking Stick paced up and down a few times and then said: 'I know a way to remove the egg from your hand.'

Kaggen jumped up. 'You must tell me!' he cried out, and grabbed the Walking Stick.

The Walking Stick looked very smug and said: 'I do not have to tell you anything.'

Kaggen let go of the Walking Stick: 'Please tell me. I will do anything.' The Walking Stick first made Kaggen promise that he would never steal Ostrich's eggs again, and then whispered in his ear what he should do. Kaggen could have jumped for joy! 'Hooray! Thank you, my friend. I will go right away.' And with that, Kaggen ran off.

The Bag turned to the Walking Stick: 'What did you tell Kaggen?'

The Walking Stick chuckled and answered: 'I told him that the only way to break the spell was to first return the eggs he stole from Ostrich, and then go and find the Magic Bird.'

The Bag was puzzled: 'Why are you laughing?'

The Walking Stick answered: 'Because I have tricked Kaggen. You see, it is true that the Magic Bird can help him, but he does not have to return the eggs to Ostrich to break the spell. I only said that so that Kaggen will never try and steal eggs from Ostrich again.'

The Bag also begun to laugh: 'I think Kaggen has learnt his lesson.'

When the Ostrich saw Kaggen, she shouted angrily from her nest: 'You had better not come any closer, you naughty mantis.'

Kaggen held up the Ostrich's egg and said: 'Please do not be angry, I have eaten one of your eggs, but I have come to return the other one.'

The Ostrich did not trust Kaggen. 'Is this one your tricks? Why would you do that?' she asked him.

Kaggen held up his other hand that had the silver egg stuck to it and said: 'Look what has happened to me. I am sorry that I stole your eggs, and I promise never to do it again.'

The Ostrich began to howl with laughter and said to Kaggen: 'I am happy that you are giving back my eggs, but the only one that can help you is the Magic Bird.'

When he heard these words, Kaggen knew that the Walking Stick had tricked him into giving the eggs back to the Ostrich. 'So, I did not have to give back the eggs, after all,' muttered Kaggen to himself. But it was too late. The Ostrich had grabbed the eggs and they were now safely in her nest.

And so Kaggen left the Ostrich and went off to find the Magic Bird. As he neared her nest, he heard the soft tinkling sound of the Magic Bird's wings and, to his great surprise, he saw that the silver egg had become loose and had rolled into her nest. Kaggen was scared that the Magic Bird would see him, so he quickly ran away.

That was the last time that Kaggen ever saw the Magic Bird and sometimes, when he was tempted to steal eggs from the Ostrich, he would hear the soft tinkling of the Magic Bird's wings, and would remember his promise.

Published by Struik Publishers (a division of New Holland Publishing
   (South Africa) (Pty) Ltd)
New Holland Publishing is a member of Johnnic Communications Ltd
Cornelis Struik House, 80 McKenzie Street, Cape Town 8001
86 Edgware Road, London, W2 2EA, United Kingdom
14 Aquatic Drive, Frenchs Forest, NSW 2086, Australia
218 Lake Road, Northcote, Auckland, New Zealand

www.struik.co.za

PUBLISHING MANAGER: Linda de Villiers
MANAGING EDITOR: Cecilia Barfield
EDITOR: Glynne Newlands
DESIGNER: Beverley Dodd
ILLUSTRATOR: Marjorie van Heerden
PROOFREADER: Gavin Barfield
REPRODUCTION: Hirt & Carter Cape (Pty) Ltd
PRINTING AND BINDING: Kyodo Printing Co (Singapore) Pte Ltd

ISBN 978 1 77007 226 8

10 9 8 7 6 5 4 3 2 1

www.imagesofafrica.co.za

IMAGES OF AFRICA
PHOTO LIBRARY

Over 40 000 unique African images available to purchase from our image bank at www.imagesofafrica.co.za